THE CAB CONSPIRACY

JIGS ASHAR

Srishti
PUBLISHERS & DISTRIBUTORS

Srishti Publishers & Distributors
A unit of AJR Publishing LLP
212A, Peacock Lane
Shahpur Jat, New Delhi – 110 049

editorial@srishtipublishers.com

First published in India by
Srishti Publishers & Distributors in 2023

Printed and bound in India

For Dad.

Sometime in the near future –
sometime in the recent past.

Acknowledgments

While this book may have my name as the author, it would have not been possible to present it to you without the help of many. It does not belong only to me.

Vidya. My wife. For making me seriously think that I could put a story on paper. You literally pushed me into the creative writing space, believing in me from the very beginning. And for being the first reader of all my manuscripts.

Esha. My go-to person when I hit writer's block. Your creativity and brilliant ideas have rescued my story many times when it was stuck. And for your opinions - only a daughter could have been so brutally honest with her father's work.

Ravi Subramanian. My friend and mentor. Thank you for giving me my first break as an author with *Insomnia* and *A Brutal Hand*. I climbed the wall because you gave me the ladder.

Suhail Mathur. For being the brilliant literary presence, friend and guide in my writing pursuits, and opening the doors for me. Because you also gave this book its name.

Arup and Stuti. My publishers. For accepting me wholeheartedly, advising me and for your editorial support. Also for the thoroughly professional approach in taking my dream to fruition. And for the not-so-subtle suggestion to change the book's earlier title, which could have landed us in a bit of trouble. Thank you, team Srishti.

Himali Kothari. For encouraging me to pursue writing. You saw something in those workshops, where I discovered another part of me.

Vineeta Dawra Nangia. For giving an opportunity to literary talent in the country. It was the *Times of India Write India* season of 2017 where my short stories got lauded.

Mrs Mehta. Your remark in school was buried deep in my subconscious, that came to fore only when I signed my first book contract. After reading my essay, you had told me that someday, I will write a book. Thank you for your blessings.

Baaji. My grandmother. Creativity is that precious inheritance you have left me. I know you are smiling somewhere today. And for all the stories you have told me, here is one for you.

Finally, for all my friends and readers, thank you for having this book in your hand. I hope you have as much fun reading it as I did writing it.

01

After yet another eighteen-hour day, at around 2 a.m., Mahendra Doshi finally retired to his bedroom. He still found it difficult to believe that it had been a decade since he had first assumed office. Much had been achieved, but much was yet to be done.

Doshi had a long, hot shower – one of the few luxuries he allowed himself to indulge in – and changed into a simple cotton *kurta* and *pajama*. At two-three, he looked like a much younger man, thanks to the strict discipline he maintained over his diet. Whenever possible, which was not often these days, he took a brisk walk in the lawns of his allotted residence. These walks and reading were two things he enjoyed the most; and lately, he could hardly find the time to do either. But that would change very soon, he told himself.

He felt slightly hungry, and was tempted to call for some *dal-chawal*. But the craving soon passed, after he grabbed an apple and bit into it. He was exhausted and also had an early start the next day; but, as was his habit, he went over to his desk to review his to-do list for the day. It was his routine for over fifty years now, and he could not remember a single day that he had skipped it.

He thought about his illustrious predecessors, feeling both privileged and nostalgic at the same time. Pushing his laptop aside, he opened a brown, leather-bound diary to the first page. While he was a strong advocate for using technology, in some things, he preferred to be old-school. He reviewed each item in the diary and struck off all ten points, feeling satisfied. He then tore the page from the diary, shredded it into little pieces and threw them in a bin underneath the huge desk. The diary had only a few pages left in it now; when all the pages were used up, Doshi would simply replenish it with more sheets of paper instead of ordering a new one. It was his way of signaling to his staff, who, he hoped, would follow suit in more ways than one, and cut down on wasteful expenditure.

For a few moments, Doshi stared at the fresh page in the diary, ready to make his checklist for the following day. But after a few minutes, he sighed and closed the diary. For the first time in his life, he did not need to make one. He thought about the only thing he wanted to accomplish the next day, and nodded to himself. He had made up his mind, but he was worried about the questions that would most certainly arise. He walked over to his bed and lay down, but found himself unable to sleep. For the umpteenth time that day, Doshi went over in his mind how he would handle the situation.

When the alarm went off, as usual, at 5 a.m., Mahendra Doshi, the prime minister of India, was already wide awake, not having slept a wink that night.

02

The Serpent buttoned his winter overcoat and put on his hat. The cold air cut through his thick overcoat, freezing up his uncovered face and he wished he had worn an extra layer of clothing. He was amazed at how quickly the temperature had dipped, even though the sun was shining bright.

He looked around him at the vast expanse of desolate wilderness of white steppe, interrupted only by the mountain beyond. The Serpent had always wondered what it would be like to be here. The name of the place, he thought, was apt – Pole of Inaccessibility. As the name implied, it is the point farthest from any sea or ocean in the world – at least 2500 kilometres – in any direction. The Pole of Inaccessibility is located in China, east of its border with Kazakhstan, and is amongst one of the least populated areas of the world. *And this is in China – a country with over 1.5 billion people!* The Serpent shook his head and smiled at the irony.

He looked at his watch, and realized he had only an hour left until the meeting. A meeting he had called for. He turned around and started to walk back to the car waiting for him. The polished surface of the Audi A8 reflected the final rays of the setting sun. When he was a few metres away, a uniformed chauffeur stood in attention, and held open the rear door for the Serpent, who acknowledged the young Chinese valet.

Right before he got into the car, the Serpent turned around. Just beyond the Pole of Inaccessibility, where the Tian Shan range of mountains branched into two, history was being written, and the Serpent was determined to see himself among those responsible for writing this new chapter in history. He was ready to do whatever it took to see it done.

And for that, the prime minister must die.

03

The World Economic Forum, or WEF, is a non-governmental organization headquartered in Switzerland. Founded in 1971, the WEF hosts an annual summit every January in Davos, a mountain town in the Swiss alps. Officially a conference, the summit attracted over three thousand corporate bosses, politicians from across the globe and journalists for the networking opportunities it provided over a period of five days. Each year, the event has a theme around which the sessions and discussions revolve. This year, the theme was 'Partnering for Economic Growth'.

Prime Minister Mahendra Doshi, who had flown into Zurich that morning from New Delhi, along with the Indian delegation, took a chartered private jet to Davos. When the Gulfstream G200 landed at Davos, light snow had begun to fall. The Indian team crunched through the thin blanket of snow towards a convoy of four cars waiting for them at the edge of the runway. Doshi got into the first one with Jayant Goswami, the Principal Secretary of the prime minister's office, or the PMO. The rest of the delegation, all members of the ruling Indian People's Party, got into the remaining three.

A seasoned bureaucrat, Goswami was hand-picked by Doshi when he had won the mandate ten years back. Apart from discharging his secretarial functions, Goswami, with his astute sense of Indian politics, was a trusted advisor to Doshi. As soon as the car started, Goswami handed over a dossier to Doshi. Doshi went through the notes on his way to the hotel. He was to deliver the inaugural speech at the event. A weathered politician, he spent no more than five minutes on the ten-page document. He had held the distinction of giving the keynote speech, including this year's, thrice in his political career. The first one was when he had just assumed his office.

His mind was preoccupied with the meeting he planned to have that evening with his core team, including his political advisors and senior party members. After weeks of trying to find the ideal opportunity to have the discussion, when he saw the Davos invitation at his desk, he had made up his mind. This way, he could hand-pick the people to whom he wanted to break the news first. And the isolated setting of Davos offered a valuable chance to meet his team away from the frenetic pace of work back in India.

'Everything okay, sir?' Goswami asked, sensing that Doshi was not his usual self.

'All okay, my friend,' Doshi smiled at the man who had served him loyally for ten years. Goswami smiled back. But from the prime minister's body language, he was certain something important was bothering him.

***

After a smooth twenty-minute ride, the Indian convoy eased into the driveway of Hotel Seehof. Most of the rooms in the hotel were booked for the heads of states and their teams; with the remaining few taken up by various top corporate bosses. The rest of the attendees had made their arrangements in other hotels close by. As a rule, no journalists were allowed in the non-conference areas, and none of them could find accommodation in the Seehof during the summit days. For the summit's organizing and planning team, this made the logistics and security arrangements easier.

Someone in the planning team had once raised some concern about a 'concentration risk' – with so many world leaders under one roof. What if terrorists struck at the hotel? And while it was acknowledged as a valid point, pretty much nothing was done about it, except that since then, the invitations to the event carried a disclaimer absolving the organizers of any liability should an untoward incident take place due to a security lapse.

The bigger problem, however, for the hotel management, was something else. A week before the event, they would receive a list of the food preferences of dignitaries from around the world. The hotel had to keep a stock of food items as varied as it could get. The only solace was that politicians had a long public career, leading to infrequent changes to the attendee list, and their dietary choices were well known in advance by the hotel staff. Almost every world leader was accompanied by a personal chef, who wanted access to the hotel kitchen. But over the years, things on this front, too, were running smoothly. The only hiccup had happened three years ago, when mistakenly, the Russian emissary's order of *beef stroganoff* was sent to the Indian delegate's room. The hotel manager, when he heard about the goof-up, rushed to apologize to the Indian politician's room. He was especially worried as the Indian minister had played a leading role in banning beef in many states in India. He was already thinking of how he would manage the backlash when he knocked at the minister's door. To his utter surprise, and relief, the minister, who had polished off the plate, calmly dismissed the bungle with, 'I am okay with it when I am *not* in India.'

As soon as Doshi stepped out of the car, a crowd of journalists that had gathered at the hotel's entrance, started clicking pictures. The snow was coming down heavily now, with the sun mostly hidden behind a gray sky. A special area was cordoned off for the press, who respected the boundary. Another gathering of civilians was chanting 'Doshi, Doshi' from the sidelines. Doshi's popularity had grown immensely amongst Indians who lived overseas, especially in his second term as prime minister. His powerful oratory skills and ability to connect with people were quite unmatched in the current crop of world leaders. Doshi used this ability to the fullest, both in India and on the world stage.

And today, he knew, this gift would be tested to its limit in front of his own team.

Doshi stood at the entrance of the hotel, smiling and waving to the gathering. He even stepped forward and shook hands with an elderly gentleman in the crowd. His head of security, though quite used to Doshi's unique style, frowned in worry. Even in a relatively safe place like Switzerland, he did not let his guard slip. He heaved a sigh of relief when Doshi finally entered the hotel lobby, where things would be much easier to control.

'Goswami,' Doshi called out just before he went to his room, 'gather everyone in my room for a meeting tonight, right after the event.'

***

'May I interrupt you, gentlemen?' Goswami politely cut in, seizing an opportune pause in the conversation.

'Goswami, my friend, come and join us,' said Namit Jha, the home minister of India. He was chatting with Lalit Mahajan, one of the senior-most members of the Indian People's Party. Mahajan smiled at Goswami, and gave him a fatherly pat on the back.

Jha and Mahajan were having a cup of tea during the break before the last session of the day. Goswami conveyed Doshi's message about the meeting he wanted to have in his room afterwards.

'Meeting? Why?' Jha questioned. He found it strange that in Davos, where they were surrounded by politicians from all over the world, Doshi wanted to spend time with the Indian representatives. His itinerary would normally be packed with back-to-back meetings with his counterparts from around the world.

In response, Goswami simply shrugged his shoulders.

'You must know what this is all about?' Jha asked Mahajan, looking intently at his senior colleague.

Mahajan only smiled and shook his head innocently. While he had no idea why they were called, he wanted to give the impression that he probably knew the reason. He was, after all, the senior-most party member, and, along with Doshi, had risen in the party ranks. Known for his sharp political acumen, Mahajan had been a mentor to most of the senior party members over the years. Although he had never held any government office directly, he was known to be one of the most powerful people in Indian politics.

'We will be there,' Mahajan confirmed.

'Thank you,' muttered Goswami and proceeded in the direction of the Indian finance minister.

***

Mahendra Doshi took one final look at himself in the mirror before he started to leave for the last session of the first day – a presentation on the Belt and Road Initiative, or BRI, by the President of China, Xi Liu. As he was about to open the door of his suite to step out, there was a knock. Trusting that the person at the door would have cleared security, Doshi opened the door, and for a moment, was taken aback to see the visitor.

'President Liu, what a pleasant surprise!' Doshi exclaimed, warmly hugging the President of the People's Republic of China. Most world leaders were now familiar with Doshi's style of greeting, although a lot of them, like Liu, still reciprocated awkwardly. 'I was about to come down for your session.'

'You look well, my friend,' Liu said, smiling warmly at Doshi, and walked inside.

Doshi gestured to a sofa in the living area of the lavish suite, where the two leaders sat down across from each other. While puzzled by the Chinese President's surprise visit, Doshi managed to keep a straight face, waiting for Liu to lead the discussion.

'You know, China and India are similar in more ways than

one,' Liu started, doing away with further pleasantries. 'We are amongst the fastest growing economies, our people are young and talented, and most importantly, we are great neighbours.'

Doshi nodded in agreement, waiting for the President to segue to the real discussion.

'I will come straight to the point. I have come to appeal to you, yet again, to partner with China on the BRI,' Liu said bluntly.

Doshi had half-suspected that this was the motive behind Liu's surprise visit. The BRI was the topic of Liu's presentation that evening. He was sure he would have to deal with this discussion during the Davos trip. *The sooner the better*, he thought.

The BRI, announced in 2013 by Liu, was a China-led effort to build a vast network of highways and railroads ("Belt") and shipping routes ("Road"), supported by hundreds of new plants, pipelines and company towns in scores of countries. The end objective of the BRI project is to link China's coastal factories and rising consumer class with Central, Southeast and South Asia; with the Gulf States and the Middle East; with Africa; and with Russia and all of Europe, by way of a global grid of land and sea routes.

Till date, China had not published any official map of the Belt and Road routes nor listed any of the approved projects, and while it was estimated that more than a hundred countries were involved in some form, there was no exact count of participating nations. Whatever be the exact number of countries and projects, the audacity of the plan was something never attempted before in the history of mankind. It would, without any doubt, catapult China as the number one economic power in the world, challenged by none.

But the BRI was just the tip of the iceberg. On one hand, China presented and marketed the huge economic benefits that the BRI would bring to the world and its partner nations. On the other, China's real motive, however, was to establish economic, but mainly political, dominance over smaller, cash-strapped nations.

The mathematics of this arrangement was fairly simple. For a rapid rise in economic growth, huge investments in infrastructure would have to be made in a poor nation. As the nation could not possibly afford to make such a heavy investment, China would offer a loan. Given the terms of the loan, invariably, the country would not be able to service it in a few years' time. The price of settling the debt? Compromising national sovereignty and self-respect by giving away strategic leverage to China.

Many recent examples substantiated this theory. In East Africa, China had established its military presence, at its first overseas naval base in Djibouti. Trapped in a debt crisis after borrowing billions of dollars on a BRI project, Djibouti was left with no choice but to lease land for the military base to China for a paltry sum as annual rent. Similarly, Sri Lanka had to hand over the port of Hambantota to China on a 99-year lease in 2017 after struggling to pay debts incurred from its construction executed by Chinese companies. Beijing had also stepped up its infrastructure investments in Bangladesh, Nepal, Pakistan and the Maldives, raising concerns about its growing influence in India's neighbourhood. Post the massive economic impact of the Covid-19 pandemic, many of these countries were hurtling towards default, Zambia being the first African country to fail since the beginning of the pandemic.

Internationally, countries were slowly waking up to China's sketchy practices, veiled behind the 'economic partnership' narrative. The International Monetary Fund (IMF) had issued a caution that Chinese loans were promoting unsustainable debt burdens. India, too, had publicly denounced the BRI as an opaque, neo-colonial initiative meant to advance China's geopolitical agenda. Studies conducted by leading global economic institutions estimated that China, through these means, had become the world's largest official creditor surpassing traditional, official lenders such as the World Bank, the IMF, or all OECD creditor governments combined.

Using India's strategic geographical position for both the Belt and the Road, China's sub-continental ambition would be fulfilled not only much earlier than the planned completion of the BRI in 2049, but it would also bring in hundreds of billions of dollars annually. Hence, India's participation in the BRI was critical for China.

Doshi remembered the previous two occasions when China had proposed a partnership with India on the BRI; and on both occasions, India had refused – first through the commerce ministry and then the diplomatic channels. Not to be deterred, China had also used non-diplomatic means to further its BRI ambitions. The recent clash between the two neighbours' armed forces in the Galwan valley was a case in point. The border skirmish had been initiated by China, not because they were pushing a border claim with India, but because they trying to secure a key route for the BRI. The sourness between the two countries, over the BRI, reached a flashpoint when the Indian Chief of Defense Staff cautioned India's neighbouring countries about China's true intentions in no uncertain terms, and urged them to rethink their foreign policy in regards to China. Now, Liu was playing his final card – an unplanned, one-on-one meeting with the prime minister himself.

'President Liu, you know our stand on this,' Doshi said politely, but firmly. 'For India, alignment with our national priorities is most critical. Our territorial integrity has to be respected. The economic priorities come second.'

Doshi did not elaborate further. And Liu did not seek any further explanation. He understood what Doshi was talking about. As a part of the BRI, China had signed a sixty-billion-dollar agreement with Pakistan, to develop the China-Pakistan

Economic Corridor (CPEC), which would be China's gateway to the Middle East and Africa.

For India, the CPEC project was much more than an economic arrangement. The CPEC passed through Pakistan-occupied Kashmir (PoK), a contentious, almost explosive issue between India and Pakistan, which India could not overlook.

'Is there a way we can move forward on this?' Liu asked Doshi one final time.

Doshi came straight to the point. 'We are good neighbours, Mr President. There has been no impact of your partnership with Pakistan on our bilateral trade relations. In fact, trade has only increased over the last few years between India and China. But on the BRI, our stand is clear – unless you call off the CPEC project, India will not participate in the BRI.'

There was complete silence in the room as the two giants of world politics stared at each other, unblinking. For Liu, the CPEC was not just an infrastructural project. It was about control and power. Pakistan was an ideal candidate for China's debt-trap politics, and CPEC was the first step towards ultimate dominance over the failed state. It was only a matter of time until China used its leverage to build a naval base next to Gwadar port. And the ultimate prize for China? Karachi... No, China could not revoke the CPEC.

'Okay, I understand. I am sorry we are not able to agree on this,' Liu sighed. Glancing at his watch, he said, 'It is time for my presentation.' He smiled, shook hands with Doshi, and left the suite, as unceremoniously as he had come.

Doshi did not miss the hatred in Liu's cold-eyed gaze.

04

About 130 kilometres from the Pole of Inaccessibility, just across from China's border with Kazakhstan, is a village called Khorgos, with a population of less than a thousand. Most of the world does not know of its existence. Except, of course, the Chinese. Until the previous year, even the Serpent had not heard of it; it was mind-boggling to think of the role Khorgos was going to play in the global economy in the not-so-distant future. Incidentally, there is also a city called Korgas (sometimes also referred to as Khorgos) on the Chinese side of the border.

As the Audi sped towards the China-Kazakhstan border, the Serpent pondered over the political turmoil taking root across the world, post Russia's invasion of Ukraine. America with its waning global influence. The post-Brexit economics for the UK and the European Union. Violence in South America and Africa. The volatile politics of North Korea and Iran. The Israel-Hamas war. And at home, India's worsening relations with Pakistan. Amongst this, the Covid-19 pandemic had taken a heavy economic toll on all nations. And while the world was busy fighting these inconsequential battles as per the Serpent, China was working stealthily to become a true economic super-power with the BRI. When he had first heard of the plan – and he was quite sure he was not privy to even ten percent of the *real* plan – he was left stunned at its incredible scale. It would change the global economic hierarchy forever.

He had travelled from India to see for himself how the BRI was taking shape, and what he had to offer to the Chinese. And of course, he would also extract his pound of flesh. That's the reason he had arranged the meeting.

The Serpent's thoughts were interrupted as he felt the car slow down. They were descending through a village, and the border sentry post was within view in a valley, which, in contrast to the to the sea of brown they had covered so far, was full of greenery. Within minutes, they drove into Korgas, where suddenly, a cluster of high-rises came into view, looking impressive, but completely out of place. And just beyond them was the border checkpoint. The Serpent began to unzip a leather folder to take out his passport, but the officer at the post waved them through into Kazakhstan.

Almost immediately, the Serpent could see the difference at this side of the border, as the car approached Khorgos. It seemed like any other village. He passed through the central square, which was dominated by a multi-coloured mosque with the curved rim of a Chinese pagoda. There were three taxis parked outside the central market, which was erected in shipping containers. Once out of the 'busy' area, the Serpent got the first glimpse of what he had come there to see. The gantry cranes of the new dry port – soon to be the largest port of its kind in the world.

The Serpent smiled in satisfaction. Now, Khorgos looked like the work-in-progress hub that he had heard of. Strategically located at the junction of the world's soon-to-be-largest national economy and its largest landlocked country, Khorgos was poised to become the next Dubai. And even more prosperous, in fact.

It was dark when the car stopped at the railway exchange station in Khorgos Gateway. As the Serpent alighted from the car, he was once again hit by the cold wind. He stretched, rubbing his hands for warmth, and hurried towards the station. The Gateway connected Kazakhstan to China by rail, where at that moment, a transfer of goods from one train to another was taking place. As a former member of the Soviet bloc, Kazakhstan used Russia's wider gauge, which means whenever cargo crossed in or out of China, it needed to be transferred to different wagons.

The Serpent entered the waiting room situated on the ground floor of the only building at the railway platform. The Serpent felt warm and comfortable immediately. Stiff from the car journey, he preferred to pace up and down the small room. He had another thirty minutes to kill. Just then, the wooden door to the waiting room opened and a smiling face peeped in. It was the chauffeur. He came in with a bottle of water and a cold sandwich wrapped in plastic.

'Thank you,' the Serpent said as he accepted the refreshments. The chauffeur bowed, and without a word, left the room as quickly as he had come. As the Serpent bit into the cold chicken sandwich, he thought about the risk he was undertaking by meeting with the Chinese. But he had waited long for the opportunity, and after the prime minister's closed-door meeting in Davos two months ago, he knew the time was right. The very next day after Doshi's announcement, the Serpent had met the Chinese at the summit and tested the waters. They were keen, as he had known they would be. Since then, the Serpent had spent every waking hour formulating his plan, until he had perfected it to the minutest detail.

Today, he would set his plan in motion.

05

'Did you notice he did not mention India even once in his speech?' remarked Namit Jha, moving his hand over his balding pate, referring to President Liu's just-concluded session. After the session, the Indian delegation had gathered in prime minister Doshi's suite in response to his summons.

'Is that really a bad thing? I think Liu played it smart. If he had mentioned India, it would have reminded the audience of India's denouncement of the BRI, and likely put off a few potential investors,' said Lalit Mahajan. Jha nodded in agreement, as did Goswami. Doshi smiled and raised his coffee cup at Mahajan. *What would I have done without the wise man's counsel?* He wondered.

'I agree, it was a calculated omission,' added Devika Naidu, the finance minister.

Apart from being the first female finance minister, Devika Naidu, at forty-four, also held the distinction of being the youngest finance minister to take oath. She had quit her job as the chief economist of a leading multinational bank in London to foray into Indian politics as a part of Doshi's top team in his second term. That was almost five years back. Her predecessor, a brilliant financial mind, had passed away young, in his mid-fifties, just at the onset of the previous elections. The loss had left a big void in the Indian People's Party (IPP) leadership, and Doshi had lost a close confidant and friend. He had closely followed Devika's meteoric rise and even read her books, and when the time came, he offered her the job. An offer she was only too glad to accept.

It was almost 10 p.m. when Jha said, 'Bhai Goswami, are you not going to offer us dinner?' Goswami looked at Doshi, who nodded slightly. 'Right away, Jha,' Goswami replied. He was relieved Jha had raised the point; he was famished, as he was sure the others were, too. Only Jha could afford to be so casual when Doshi was around. Doshi and Jha went back a long way, more than twenty-five years. Doshi was the chief ministerial candidate of the IPP from Gujarat, and Jha was the leader of the opposition party. When the results were announced, Doshi was short of majority, and Jha had offered him his party's support. Doshi witnessed first-hand how ruthless Jha could be when he had to get a minister over to his side – he would stop at nothing. After Doshi became the chief minister, for the first of his three terms, he offered Jha a key position in his government. Jha accepted and the two had been inseparable ever since. Doshi, who had never married and had no immediate family, considered Jha his younger brother. Jha, in return, worshipped Doshi.

Goswami dialled room service and said into the handset, 'Please send the dinner now.'

'Very impressive, Goswami. Everything planned to perfection, as always,' chuckled Jha. The rest joined in the laughter. Goswami smiled sheepishly. Just then, there was a knock on the door.

'Wow, that was quick. Did you have someone wait outside the room with the dinner?' Jha continued the banter. More laughter followed.

Goswami opened the door. 'Good evening, everyone,' said the newcomer, as he walked in and shook hands with everyone, bending to touch the feet of Doshi and Mahajan, as a mark of respect. He took a seat next to Jha, where Goswami was sitting earlier. Jha frowned in annoyance, and turned his attention to his mobile.

'When did you arrive, Sanjay?' Devika asked first.

'Late afternoon,' smiled the young chief minister of Maharashtra, Sanjay Adhikari. Adhikari had just turned fifty, and was one of the young brigades, along with Devika, in Doshi's government. He had held several important positions in the state government of the IPP in Maharashtra before he was given the top job in the state by Doshi.

Adhikari's appointment as chief minister of the highest revenue generating state in India had raised quite a few eyebrows in the Indian political circle, including several objections by IPP's senior party members, even Mahajan. Jha was also one of the naysayers, as he was in favour of someone more senior, and was quite vocal about his opinion to Doshi. The prime minister, however, went ahead with his decision regardless. And Adhikari had not let him down.

Adhikari cut through all the noise of religion and caste-based politics of his predecessors, and made 'development' his main agenda. He had accurately read the change in the mindset of Indian voters – all they wanted was employment, education and a better quality of life. Adhikari went full-steam ahead with his developmental agenda. Within a year, his critics across political parties fell short of finding weak links in Adhikari's governance that they could leverage against him politically. And over the last five years, Adhikari's stature within the IPP, and Maharashtra's rise as the number one state in India, on the economic front, had grown at a meteoric rate.

Dinner was served. Goswami, observant as ever, had taken care of the likes and dislikes of the group, and had particularly arranged for at least one favourite dish of everyone in the room. Political gossip occupied most of the conversation time, and Doshi mainly listened. He was very careful with his choice of words, not letting anything slip out that may be unworthy of his office.

After dinner, the group was settled in the living area again, when Doshi said, 'Friends, I have an announcement to make.'

***

There was stunned silence in the room, which, just a few moments ago, was boisterous and lively. Everyone looked expectantly at

Doshi. Even Goswami, who would normally be in the know of the prime minister's plans, was caught unawares. Doshi scanned the faces of the people he had worked with for a long time, and began.

'Friends, thanks to all of you, and everyone in the IPP, our party has done very well in the last decade. From a party that could barely manage to form the government without support from our allies, we have consolidated our position to being almost... invincible. I have served our country as the prime minister for two terms now. And, I am happy to be surrounded by such strong leadership, who can take the country – and the party – forward.'

At this, everyone straightened up, half-expecting what was coming. Doshi smiled and continued, 'I have decided not to contest the upcoming elections.'

'What?' Jha and Mahajan cried out together. Goswami sat expressionless, staring at Doshi. Adhikari and Devika exchanged a questioning glance. 'The elections are just seven months away... why do you need to? We will lose if you drop out now!' Jha stuttered.

'No, we won't. I will continue to campaign for the party. But I will not be the prime ministerial candidate.' He paused, then added calmly, 'I have decided to retire from active politics.'

'Retire? You are too young to do that!' Mahajan retorted. The rest of the team stared speechlessly at Doshi.

'I am seventy-three.'

'Exactly what I am saying – that's young in politics.'

Doshi laughed good-humouredly.

'Mahendra, I am not joking,' Mahajan said. He had never addressed the prime minister by his first name, except when they were alone. Doshi was not offended though. He knew his friend was trying to prevail on him to change his decision.

'But we need your leadership and guidance,' protested Devika. Adhikari nodded vigorously in agreement.

'I will always be around for you all and the party. I just don't want to stand for office,' Doshi asserted.

Mahajan sighed and shook his head. 'And the public? They want *you* as their prime minister – what about that?'

'The public wants a good, honest leader – someone who will work for their betterment. And I have chosen someone to succeed me as the prime ministerial candidate.'

If Doshi's decision to retire had shaken the team, this statement of his stunned them further. Jha looked at Mahajan, trying to figure out if he knew something, but he saw that he was just as surprised.

After a long pause, Doshi smiled and announced, 'Sanjay Adhikari will be the new face of the party to be the next prime minister.'

06

Rajan Naidu was not interested in the speeches and the formal sessions of the WEF summit. He had come on a paid invite to Davos only to network with the corporate honchos and government officials, especially the ones from Africa. He saw in Africa an enormous opportunity to expand his hotel business. Born to a middle-class family in Hyderabad, Rajan had completed his post-graduation from the reputed Indian Institute of Management in Bangalore, after which he joined a multi-national FMCG company. Three years later, he married his batchmate from IIM, Devika.

Devika, who was working with a foreign bank in Mumbai as an economist, got a job offer to be the chief economist of the bank. The catch? Relocation to London, where the bank was headquartered. Rajan quit his job and moved with her to London. Within six months of moving, he had opened his first Indian restaurant in the queen's city. It was an instant hit. Within a year, Rajan managed to add three more to the chain, including one in Delhi, India. While his restaurant business was on an upswing, the real boom came four years back, when he partnered with a leading Russian hotel chain to open a five-star hotel in Delhi. It was the Russian conglomerate's first foray into India and most of the launch was handled by Rajan. Until Devika became the finance minister, Rajan was more well-known than her in India, due to his meteoric rise from a middle-class background to a young, ambitious achiever.

They had been in London for a little over ten years when Doshi's offer came, inviting Devika to be the first ever female finance minister of India. Rajan was only too happy to move back with her, as he was looking to expand his hotel business in India and Africa.

'Really? Adhikari?' he asked Devika when she told him about Doshi's announcement. They were sipping wine in their room. It was after 1 a.m. that Devika returned from Doshi's meeting; Rajan was awake, already on his fourth glass, and waiting to hear what the prime minister had to say. *This news changes everything – it is* not *going as planned,* he thought.

'You should have seen the victorious smirk on that bastard Adhikari's face when he looked at me,' Devika said, her voice quavering with anger. Her eyes were moist, and Rajan hugged her. He was still thinking about how his plans had been impacted with this, and what he could do to get them back on track.

'Why not me?' Devika sobbed in his arms.

Exactly my point. Why not you? Rajan thought. He had to do something about it.

***

The phone rang for quite some time before Manjiri, fast asleep, heard it and picked up. She saw *'Hubby'* flashing on the screen. It was 4:30 a.m., and unusual for him to call at this time, knowing the time difference between India and Switzerland. 'Are you alright?' was the first thing she asked when she finally answered the phone.

'Everything is fine. Sorry to wake you up, but I couldn't wait,' Sanjay Adhikari said to his wife of twenty years.

Manjiri screamed in delight when she heard the news. Adhikari, much amused, waited patiently at the other end for his wife to calm down. He himself wanted to react in a similar manner when Doshi had announced his name. However pleasant, it was a complete jolt out of the blue. His hard work and 'politics of development' had paid the ultimate dividend. Of course, Delhi was going to be a different ball-game. But in the words of his favourite actor, Sean Connery, 'Nothing like a good challenge to bring out the best in a man.'

'No, no, everything is fine... sorry,' Adhikari heard Manjiri say to someone. He then heard a door close.

'What was that?' he asked.

'Oh, nothing. It was Dalvi. He just came to check if I was okay,' Manjiri replied sheepishly.

Adhikari laughed. Manjiri's gleeful shriek must have drawn Dalvi's attention, prompting him to check in on her. Manmohan Dalvi was Adhikari's head of security and over the years, had become a dear friend as well. Dalvi normally accompanied Adhikari on his trips, except this time around; at Adhikari's request, he had stayed back to watch over Manjiri and Aashi at home in Mumbai. Aashi was their only child, who would be turning seventeen in a few months. Adhikari remembered how difficult it was for her – the change of schools every two or three years.

And the swiftness with which he came to check on Manjiri reaffirmed, yet again, the faith Adhikari had in him.

'So, when will the official announcement be made?' Manjiri asked.

'Not sure about that, but it should be in the next week or so.'

'Aashi will be thrilled when she gets to know.'

'Alright then, you go back to sleep. I'll call you later,' Adhikari concluded.

'I am not in Davos, Mr Prime Minister. It is already 5 a.m. here,' Manjiri teased him.

'Oh, yes, I completely forgot. We will celebrate when I am back,' Adhikari chuckled, and hung up. He opened the minibar and took out a can of beer. He was an occasional drinker, and hated to drink alone. But today was a special occasion. He took a large swig of the cold ale, and relaxed on the comfortable arm-chair, thinking about the future.

God, I hope Doshi doesn't change his mind, was his last thought as he drifted to sleep.

07

'I refuse to believe that you did not know about this!' Jha said in a raised voice.

'Believe me, I had no idea he would be making such an announcement,' Mahajan replied. He was having breakfast with Jha in the outdoor seating area of the Seehof.

It was very early, not yet seven, and most of the guests were still in their rooms. The area would be packed by eight, as most of the crowd would be down for breakfast to make it in time for the conference starting at nine.

'I have *nothing* to look forward to now,' Jha scoffed, and moved his hand over his beard, caressing it. He had clearly not slept the previous night; the dark circles under his eyes seemed more pronounced.

Mahajan shook his head, and tried to calm down his agitated colleague. 'You are one of our brightest stars in the party. Just wait for the right opportunity,' the old man advised.

'And work under a newbie? No way!'

'We all work for the country and the party,' Mahajan said, as he sipped his orange juice.

'I am not going to be side-lined by anyone – always thrown aside for others... I am not *you*!' Jha hissed, squinting at Mahajan, raising his finger at him.

Mahajan's face contorted with rage, and his eyes blackened. 'Don't you dare...,' he leaned forward.

Jha did not say anything further, fuming in silence. He emptied three sachets of sugar in his cup of tea, and stirred absent-mindedly. Normally, Mahajan would have reprimanded him, but today, he thought it was best to leave him to his own devices, and he, too, wanted to be left alone. He had his own demons to fight.

Jha had survived a health scare two years ago; a heart attack that was, fortunately, not fatal as he was rushed to the hospital in time. Both Mahajan and Doshi had time and again warned Jha against his increasing weight and especially, his unhealthy eating habits. But Jha would always laugh it off. 'We only live once' was his casual comeback to their advice.

'Good morning, gentlemen. May I join you?' Goswami called out as he walked towards their table and pulled out a chair.

'Someone is very happy,' remarked Jha sarcastically, without looking up, before taking a sip of the now-cold tea.

'No, I am not... I mean,' Goswami started, clearly flustered, looking at Jha and then at Mahajan.

Mahajan had, by now, regained his composure; he just raised both his hands calmly, in a bid to diffuse the tension at the table. 'So, Goswami, what are the key meetings for today?' he asked.

'Sure, let me see,' Goswami said, as he referred to his smartphone, and took Mahajan through the day's itinerary. Mahajan noticed the cold shoulder Goswami gave Jha through the rest of the discussions. He also did not miss the enraged look in Jha's eyes as he looked at Adhikari, who waved out at them from a distance, as he walked in with Doshi.

'I should get going,' Goswami said, and left.

***

'Come, join us,' Doshi called out to Goswami as he was walking by their breakfast table. Adhikari smiled and gestured to a chair to his left.

'Congratulations once again,' Goswami said as he sat down, looking at Adhikari.

'Goswami has been invaluable to me, Sanjay, as I am sure, he will be to you,' Doshi said, patting Goswami's shoulder.

Goswami gave a half-smile at the compliment. *Until the time came to reward me, when I was forgotten.*

'I am sure,' Sanjay said, 'much like I have Raut and Pawar.'

'Well, national politics is a different ball-game, as you will see,' Goswami could not help commenting. He was almost as senior as Doshi when it came to years of experience, nowhere as 'raw' as Adhikari's two lackeys.

'Yes, that's true,' Doshi agreed. 'I think the main point is that all of us need a solid support system to discharge our duties to the nation. Alone, we cannot survive in politics.' He cleverly generalized the discussion rather than letting it stray into sensitive territory.

Goswami stared at the glass of water kept in front of him, and reflected on his situation. *And yet, here I am, fighting for my survival.* In many countries, a formal role of *Deputy Prime Minister* existed, which, in terms of responsibilities, was exactly the same as the Principal Secretary's in India. And more often than not, the deputy prime minister succeeded the prime minister; it was a very clear succession plan. Doshi had himself spoken about this similarity many times to him, but when it came to the announcement...

Goswami shook his head slowly, determined to do something about it.

08

The Serpent heard the train whistle and stepped out of the waiting room onto the platform. The freight train was ready to start its 286 kilometres' journey, connecting Khorgos to the Chinese city of Yining, ultimately ending at Jinghe. There were three daily freight services, along with a passenger line that ran overnight.

There were eight freight wagons connected to the locomotive. Looking completely out of place, a passenger coach, much longer than normal, was connected to the chain at the end of the wagons. There were four armed guards on the platform, two each at the doors of the coach. The Serpent walked towards the rear entrance, and the guards stationed there saluted as he boarded the coach. Another armed guard, waiting inside, motioned to him to follow him. He walked along the side corridor that connected the compartments along the body of the coach, until the guard stopped at a compartment and knocked on its door once. The Serpent could hear someone saying something in Chinese, and the guard bowed and pushed open the door. The Serpent entered the compartment.

He smiled when he saw Chen Jintao, the foreign minister of the People's Republic of China (PRC). Jintao got up from the arm-chair, smiling warmly, and shook the Serpent's hand. His straight, black hair was combed back, and he had almost no eyebrows, which made his forehead look abnormally large above his dark eyes. The Serpent smiled back.

Jintao, at sixty-seven, was a veteran politician, and had risen to be amongst the top leaders of the Communist Party of China (CPC). His proximity to the Chinese president was well-known, and he was often the person Liu turned to for carrying out 'sensitive operations', as he liked to call them. While Jintao was not yet a part of the seven-member Politburo Standing Committee of the CPC, he was considered as powerful as any of its members, both within and outside China.

Jintao was the brain behind the systemic prosecution of the Uyghur Muslims in China. Since 2016, over a million Uyghurs had been detained in 're-education camps', a term coined by Jintao himself. The main purpose of the camps? Forced adherence to the CPC ideology. Voluntary departure from the camps was not possible and detention lasted for a minimum period of twelve months, depending on how the inmates fared in the Chinese ideology tests.

The families of the detained alleged torture by the Chinese inside the camps – a claim refuted time and again by the government. In spite of repeated efforts by the Human Rights Commissions across the world, including United Nations' reports, the unlawful detention continued unchecked. Recently, there were reports that hundreds of detainees had gone 'missing', an allegation rubbished by Jintao.

Jintao was also a key member of the BRI leadership in China, working directly with Liu. He was an astute reader of international politics and knew what levers had to be pulled to get strategic countries to partner with China. He was a part of Liu's delegation in Davos, and when the Serpent had reached out to him with the possibility of a deal, he had seized the opening. Getting India to change its stance would surely fast-track him to become the eighth member of the Politburo Standing Committee.

Jintao led the Serpent to the plush leather armchair next to his in the lounge area. The Serpent saw that three compartments of the train were combined into one, and the interiors were luxurious. Next to the lounge area was a bar, that opened through a glass door into the kitchen. The Serpent could see there was nobody in the kitchen. To the right of the compartment, a door led into the last cabin. The door was closed, and the Serpent surmised the small adjacent room was full of armed guards and security personnel accompanying Jintao.

Jintao signalled to the guard at the door, who, at once, bowed and walked to the bar. He returned with two crystal glasses, which he placed on the table. He promptly returned again with a bottle of *Baijiu*, a local distilled alcoholic beverage.

'It tastes like vodka, only better,' Jintao told the Serpent, who was scrutinizing the bottle suspiciously. Jintao dismissed the guard, and filled the two glasses. He raised his, and clinked it with the Serpent's. The Serpent took a sip; it was way stronger than vodka, and his throat burned as the liquid trickled down. He coughed. *He is not made for the strong stuff,* Jintao thought, controlling his laughter.

The Serpent smiled sheepishly at Jintao. *No harm in letting him believe he is the stronger one,* he assured himself.

The train was chugging along in the darkness towards the Borohoro mountain range, one of the ranges of the Tian Shan. The Serpent imagined how strange the train would look from the outside, with just the one lit coach snaking its way up the mountain.

'So, let's get down to business,' the Serpent started, conscious of the fact that they had only about two hours to Yining, where they would part ways. Jintao would continue onwards, while the Serpent would fly out from Yining to Guangzhou, and then to New Delhi. Jintao had arranged a private chartered plane for his guest, booked in the name of a Chinese telecom company. Nobody could trace the booking to him or the Serpent. The entire trip would take less than two days, and the Serpent had made sure nobody would miss him.

'Let's start where we left off in Davos. As I understand your... proposition... you can get India to be a part of the BRI – correct?' Jintao asked.

'That's right.'

'I have two simple questions,' Jintao smiled, 'First, how do you plan to achieve that? And second, I am sure you are not doing this because you love China. So, what do you want in return?'

The Serpent gulped down the Baijiu, and poured himself another glass. He liked straight-talking. For the next ninety minutes, the Serpent explained what he had in mind. What initially seemed like an incredulous idea to Jintao, became increasingly plausible as the Serpent countered all his questions with specifics on how he could make it happen.

'So, what do you think? Any more questions?' the Serpent asked.

'I like it... I really do,' Jintao laughed and continued, 'and you have convinced me it is possible.'

'And it *is*.'

'Well, then, let's drink to that,' Jintao said and filled their glasses again.

'To us,' echoed the Serpent.

As the two men toasted, the train slowed down as it was pulled into the Yining station. It was almost midnight. The Serpent intended to be in New Delhi by morning.

'And my second question?' Jintao asked.

The Serpent locked eyes with Jintao and smiled slowly. For a brief moment, Jintao felt fear, an emotion he hadn't felt in a long time. He made a mental note never to cross paths with the man staring so intently at him. He quickly recovered his composure and smiled at the Serpent.

'Khorgos,' the Serpent replied, 'All the developmental and infrastructure contracts will have to be routed through me. I will set up the required structures for that.'

He does not want a share of the pie... he wants the pie itself. He is asking for too much, but I will deal with that later, Jintao thought.

'Agreed,' Jintao said, and shook hands with the Serpent.

'One more point,' Jintao said as the two men got up, 'for executing our plan, do you have someone in mind for the job?'

'Yes, I do... the best in business,' the Serpent replied.

09

The Netravathi Express, after covering a distance of almost 1750 kilometres from Thiruvananthapuram, chugged in at the Panvel railway station. The signal at the end of the platform turned red. It was 3:15 p.m., and the train was running five minutes behind schedule. The few passengers on the platform, who were waiting to board the train, walked forward in anticipation. Most of them were regular commuters, travelling daily to Panvel for work from Thane or Mumbai, waiting near the entrance to the general compartment. Suddenly, the quiet platform was full of life as passengers got off the train and hurried towards the exit.

The man sitting on a bench at the end of the platform glanced at his watch, and walked slowly towards his right. It was two more minutes for the train to depart after its usual five-minute halt. He adjusted the elastic waistband of his dark blue windcheater, and one more time, slid his right hand in and felt the Glock 26 in the carry holster. Zipping the windcheater, he climbed into the AC first class coach. He locked the compartment from inside, and started to walk slowly along the narrow corridor. Exactly on time, the train rolled out of the platform.

There were two coupes at the other end of the compartment that housed eight cabins in all. The attendant sat alone in the first cabin, making entries in a register. He did not look up as the man passed by. In the next cabin, an old lady was lying down on the lower berth, while her husband sat opposite her, reading a magazine. The next four cabins were empty, and so was the first coupe. The man braced himself as he opened the door to the second coupe and entered.

A well-built young man with cropped hair, wearing a half-sleeved shirt and denim jeans was seated on the lower berth next to the glass window. His right forearm was covered in a colourful tattoo. Next to him, on the seat, was a crumpled green sweater and a newspaper folded in two. He looked up briefly at the man in the blue windcheater as he entered the coupe, drew the sweater and the newspaper closer to him, and went back to staring out of the window into the wilderness.

On the berth opposite him, facing the engine, sat a woman with a child. The woman was bundled in an oversized sweater over her black *salwar kameez*. Her ponytail was ragged, and loose, and her black hair fell over her shoulders. Her face was pale and tired. She smiled nervously at the new entrant in the coupe. For a brief moment, her leaf green, sunken eyes glowed through silver-rimmed spectacles.

The man acknowledged her smile with a brief nod, and sat down next to the tattooed man. The child, a boy not older than four years, was fast asleep next to the woman. He lay down on the berth, curled up in a foetal position, with his chin tucked into his tiny chest. His hands were clasped together between the knees. A maroon purse rested between the woman's lap and the boy's head.

The man in the blue windcheater scanned the coupe for luggage; there was a large rolling suitcase underneath the berth where the woman was seated. Protruding slightly from below the berth he was sitting on, were a wheeled, black backpack and a brown duffel bag.

The train, now hurtling at top speed, swayed lightly sideways. As the man in the blue windcheater stretched his arms forward, the tattooed man flinched at the abrupt movement. He pulled a face, and took a sip of water from a bottle kept near his feet. Then he got up, grabbed the sweater and left the cabin, sliding the door shut.

Almost at once, the man in the blue windcheater leaned forward to the woman, and said, 'You must leave this cabin immediately.'

The woman, clearly taken aback, sank back further into her seat, staring blankly at the man, her mouth agape.

'Listen to me,' the man got up from his seat, 'this man is dangerous,' he said, pointing to where the tattooed man was sitting a moment ago.

The woman held her purse tightly. The child continued to sleep. 'But why?' she managed in a weak voice.

'There is no time to explain... see, I am a cop,' the man said, taking out police id-card from his pocket.

'But...' the woman started to say, her eyes darted from the man to the cabin door, where the tattooed man was standing. He had returned to the cabin, and looked suspiciously at the two. He glanced at the bags underneath the berths. His right hand moved towards the sweater he was holding in his left, when everything went dark.

***

As the train entered the 2.6 kilometres long tunnel, nobody saw the two muzzle flashes that went off in quick succession. The duration of the flash was reduced drastically by the flash suppressor; and the blast was contained by the silencer. Just two sharp swishing sounds. And the muffled thuds of the bodies hitting the carpeted floor of the cabin.

The assassin dragged the two corpses to one side of the cabin, locked the cabin door from the inside and drew the curtains shut. The train was still speeding through the darkness, when the assassin dismantled the silencer from the lightweight revolver, a Beretta 92FS. As the locomotive tore into daylight once again, the woman stashed the firearm inside her purse. She looked at the two lifeless men sprawled on the floor. Both were shot in the heart. *Not bad,* she said to herself.

She pulled out the black backpack from under the berth, unzipped it and took out a black *burqa*. She threw in her spectacles and the sweater in the bag, and donned the burqa. She felt the train slowing down and quickly glanced at her watch. It was almost time for the train to reach Thane station. *Perfect.*

Just then, the little boy stirred. Wasting no time, she took out the Beretta from her purse and pointed it at the sleeping child, but he turned over and dozed off again. She gazed at the child through the mesh screen of the burqa for a minute, ready to pull the trigger. When she was sure the child was not awake, she walked out of the cabin carrying her purse and the backpack.

Closing the door behind her, she walked towards the exit to the left of the compartment. She knew the attendant was at the other end, and didn't want him to notice her. As the train slowed down further, she became conscious of movement behind her. An old lady, who she recognized as one of the passengers, came out of the toilet that was adjacent to the corridor near the exit. The old lady stopped in front of the burqa-clad woman, giving her a bemused look. Finally, she walked towards her cabin, completely unaware that she had just saved her own life.

The train entered Thane station right on schedule at 4 p.m. The woman in the burqa got down, and disappeared into the sea of people on the platform.

10

The Lokmanya Tilak Terminus, or LTT as it is popularly known, is a major railway terminus in Mumbai. It is located between two suburban railway stations, Tilak Nagar and Kurla, in northern Mumbai. Although it was only a few minutes past 6 p.m., the city was unusually dark and muggy that evening in early April, as grey clouds blanketed the sky.

Inspector Anant Kulkarni wiped the sweat off his forehead with a handkerchief as the police car sped towards LTT. The pipeline road leading up to the terminus was crowded with pedestrians and auto-rikshaws, forcing the police car to slow down. Anant looked at the officer in the driver's seat to his right, and nodded slightly. The driver immediately turned on the siren, and almost on cue, the traffic parted, allowing the police car to speed ahead. The car screeched to a halt outside the main entrance to the terminus, its siren still wailing.

The tall, brawny policeman slammed the car door and stepped out of the damp interiors into an equally oppressive weather. He strode inside the railway complex and made his way towards platform number 5. Entry to the platform was cordoned off. The police team there was having a tough time fielding a barrage of questions from the reporters, who had already gathered at the platform. Anant passed through the barricade and paused. He then turned around, and addressed the press.

'I promise you I will give you an update as soon as I have the details,' he said in a deep baritone, as his thick moustache, covering his top lip, quivered. He stood there for a few seconds, eyeing each journalist, many of whom he had come to know personally over the years. He considered the media to be an important partner to law-enforcement, and maintained good equations with the fourth estate. Satisfied that his message was understood, he resumed walking towards the stationary Netravathi Express.

As he walked towards the train, he saw another cop with a train attendant, waiting near the AC first class coach, looking in his direction. They were obviously waiting for him. The cop saluted Anant, who acknowledged him with a quick nod.

'So, you called the police?' Anant asked the train attendant.

'Yes,' the attendant muttered weakly. Clad in a worn-out black coat and tie, he was perspiring profusely, and the weather was not the sole cause of his sweatiness.

'Relax,' Anant said, putting a reassuring hand on the man's shoulder. 'You want to take that off?' he asked, pointing to the attendant's thick coat. The grateful man did so, and led Anant inside the compartment. He walked along the passage, and motioned to a coupe. Anant opened the doors to the stench of death.

Two corpses were sprawled on the floor, their dead limbs intertwined. Blood, dried and congealed on the dead men's chests, had formed a sticky pool on the floor, disappearing under the berths. Anant gasped audibly as his eyes fell on the motionless child. Careful not to disturb the evidence, he took two steps inside the cabin and gingerly felt the boy's pulse. He heaved a sigh of relief as the boy stirred slightly at his touch. He swiftly lifted the child and rushed out of the cabin.

'Get an ambulance – now!' he yelled at the cop on the platform.

'It's on its way, sir,' the cop replied, 'forensics, too.'

'Good, seal the compartment. There was nothing else left to see there.'

Almost at the same time as Anant came out of the compartment on to the platform, he saw a team of paramedics rushing towards them, wheeling a stretcher behind them. Anant, carrying the child, hastened towards them. A young doctor took the child from Anant and laid him gently on the stretcher.

'He seems to be unconscious,' Anant explained.

'We'll take it from here, officer,' the doctor said reassuringly.

'I want to know how he is doing,' Anant told his fellow policeman, pointing to the child.

'Yes, sir.'

'So, you found the bodies when the train arrived at LTT?' Anant asked, turning his attention to the train attendant again.

'Yes, sir. I always check the cabins at the end of every journey. And when I opened that cabin, I saw...' the attendant turned pale, as his voice trailed off.

'And the boy was in the same state?'

'Yes, sir. But I could make out he was alive. I immediately called the police.'

'You did well. And that was around an hour back,' Anant said, glancing at his watch. 'Did you hear the shots? Or the sound of any scuffle?'

'Nothing, sir. I was in the first cabin. This happened in the last.'

'What about the other passengers in the compartment?'

'Sir, the train was almost empty after we passed Roha, which is normally the case. They were the only other passengers in the compartment,' the attendant said, pointing to an old couple seated on a bench almost at the end of the platform.

Anant walked towards the couple. The old man, almost completely bald except for a few stray strands of white, sat slightly hunched. His wife, almost the same age, sat beside him. Their bags – a black trolley bag and a hand-bag – were on the platform, next to the bench. A walking cane leaned on the bench next to the old man.

'Hello, I am Inspector Anant Kulkarni. Sorry to have kept you waiting,' he greeted the couple.

From his face, it was clear that the old man was exhausted. The frail lady, with neatly parted jet-black, dyed hair, smiled warmly at Anant.

'As you know, there has been an unfortunate incident. I hope you don't mind me asking a few quick questions,' Anant said politely.

The couple nodded slowly in unison.

'Did you see or hear anything that could help us?' Anant asked, squatting in front of them.

'We have nothing to say. We were in our cabin most of the time, except...' the man said, shaking his head.

'Except what?'

'Just when the train was arriving at Thane, I saw a passenger getting off... a woman...' the lady said, taking over from where her husband had left off.

'A woman... can you tell me anything more about her?'

'Nothing... she was wearing a burqa,' the old lady shook her head.

'Show me the passenger chart,' Anant told the attendant.

The railway attendant handed over a bunch of stapled sheets of paper, with the complete list of passengers. He turned the pages, and tapped on the names against the AC first class list. Anant took the list from him and studied the names. The attendant, standing by his side, leaned over and offered his comments.

'This is the woman,' he said, pointing to a name, 'she got in at Madgaon with the child.'

Anant stared at the names. *Salma Abbas, 36. Farooq Abbas, 4.* He shook his head. *Fake*, he was sure.

'So did he,' the attendant said, pointing another name. *Clement Gomes, 27.* 'The one with the tattoo,' he added.

'And the other man?'

'He... he must have boarded later... his name is not on the list... must be some error,' the attendant stuttered.

Anant frowned, and asked, 'Did you get a look at the woman anytime during the journey?'

'Not really... she had a dupatta over her head and most of her face when I went to check the tickets.'

'Anything at all to describe her?'

'She was wearing glasses... salwar-kameez, with a sweater on top... and the dupatta... one thing that struck me were her green eyes.'

'Take his statement,' Anant told his fellow cop, who was busy talking with the forensics team that had just arrived.

'Yes, sir,' the cop replied.

'Also, check the CCTV footage at Thane station. We know it was a lady in a burqa – where did she go?' Anant added.

After giving his final instructions to the police team, as Anant left the platform, a strong sense of foreboding engulfed him.

11

The woman in the burqa walked out of Thane station and patiently waited in the line for auto-rikshaws. She noticed that she was number eleven in the queue. Medusa, or M, as she was known to a very select few in international circles, had a special affinity for India. She travelled extensively for 'work', and after a series of assignments in Europe and Russia over the last decade, she was glad to be in this corner of the world.

She was not sure of her nationality; she had never met her mother. Or her father, for that matter. With her unremarkable, common features, she could pass off as from anywhere in the world. Over the years, she had mastered the art of camouflage; she could be anything she wanted. From invincible to vulnerable; heiress to a fortune to a penniless, homeless woman. That she was fluent in six languages was a blessing in her line of business. But what she disguised the best were her real intentions.

After an average academic career, she was working as a junior operations officer with the Indian embassy in Moscow, when she found her true calling. It had started simply enough – a copy of a classified file in exchange for a sum of money more than her annual salary. This had continued for a little over a year, when her Russian handler, impressed with her commitment and more importantly, lack of remorse, offered her a more 'serious' assignment. She accepted it without hesitation. Not for any cause or vendetta or becoming famous. Her motivation was very clear from the start. *Money. Lots of it.*

Over the next three months, an elaborate story was created by her recruiters - *She has fallen in love with a Russian restaurateur, and married him in an intimate ceremony.* Her supervisor in the

Indian embassy was thrilled for her and accepted her resignation, albeit reluctantly. She quit her job, but stayed back in Moscow.

A week after she resigned, in June 2006, she met Andrey Lugovoy.

St. Basil's Cathedral is the most prominent, and most visited landmark in Red Square. That Sunday afternoon, the place was thronged with people, both tourists and Muscovites. Dressed in a designer dress with a wide brim Panama hat and sunglasses, M blended right in with the tourists. As were her instructions, she kept walking slowly towards the southeast of the Square.

As she passed along the wall that the Red Square shares with the Kremlin, the crowd was thinning away. She jumped when she felt a tap on her shoulder. As she turned, she was taken aback to see Andrey Lugovoy. As the head of the ninth directorate in the KGB, that provided security to the Russian state's top officials, Andrey, surprisingly, travelled without any security detail of his own. Or so it seemed, at least. The former KGB agent, although she knew there was no 'former' with the KGB, gave her a brief of her next mission as they walked for the next thirty minutes.

'That's it?' she asked, skeptically.

'Yes.'

'I just have to go to London and take pictures of these three hotels?' she asked again, pointing to the piece of paper that was handed to her.

'For now, yes, that's all,' Andrey said, and handed her a sealed packet, 'your travel documents.'

She opened the envelope. Tickets. And a new passport – she looked at the photograph. She thought she was looking at a stranger, who only bore a resemblance to her. *But she could do that – she could make herself look like that.* She smiled.

'And remember, never try to reach me; wait for me to contact you,' he instructed, 'I'll be in touch.'

She nodded to herself, as he left as swiftly as he had come.

She saw the packet again. Only one word was written on it. *Medusa.*

She was jolted back to the present as an auto-rikshaw stopped noisily in front of her.

'Viviana mall,' she told the driver as she got in. The rickety vehicle made its way out of the busy station area quickly. It was 4:30 p.m. and the traffic was light; there was still an hour before the peak hour rush would clog the streets. She always found herself fascinated by auto-rickshaws; the way they came so close and then turned abruptly in another direction. After ten minutes, the auto wobbled its way to the eastern express highway. She knew the shopping mall was a kilometre to the left. As the auto was nearing a red light, she pretended to dial a number on her mobile.

'Have you reached?' she said, loud enough for the auto-driver to hear, 'Oh ok, I will do that. See you soon.'

'Bhaiya, please drop me here only. My fiancé is right around the corner,' she told the driver. She saw the fare meter reading at sixty-five rupees. She gave him a hundred and got down without another word, leaving the driver staring at the note, dumbfounded.

She walked back around two hundred metres and entered a public toilet she had spotted on her way. She kept a ten-rupee coin at the counter, where a bored woman was sitting, completely uninterested in her job. *Can't blame her,* M thought. She went into a stinking booth, removed her burqa and her black kameez, and neatly folded them. She took out a bright red kameez from the backpack and wore it on top of her salwar. She put the clothes she had removed into the bag and looked at herself in the small, stained mirror. She removed her green contact lenses and flushed them down the toilet. She looked at herself again. Nothing noticeable about her black-brown eyes. Satisfied, she wore her backpack and walked out on to the busy road. The woman at the counter did not notice her.

For M, it was just another day at work.

12

Anant walked into the state-of-the-art headquarters of the Anti-Terrorism Squad, the ATS, in the central Mumbai area of Chinchpokli. The promised building complex was finally commissioned and constructed the previous year, after years of deliberations and red-tapism over the budget and the location. An old mill, then defunct, was converted into the ATS headquarters, spanning over an area of around 6000 square metres. Interestingly, the exteriors of the building were left untouched, and to a casual onlooker, the structure still resembled the dilapidated mill. While the government's official statement was to give the place a look of anonymity, the ATS was in the know – the government had run out of funds. It never failed to amuse Anant.

Anant was quite popular in the squad, even though he was demanding and expected more than hundred percent from his team at all times. A fitness enthusiast, he had taken it upon himself to keep the squad members in top physical condition. Many of them, when he had joined, were lethargic and slow, preferring the comfort of their offices to being out in the field. A few years back, Anant and two of his team members had received a tip-off about a sleeper-cell operative, hiding in the slums of Dharavi. When they knocked at the door of his shanty, the man fled. The three cops pursued the man, on foot, on a hot summer afternoon. Before long, the two officers with Anant were panting. To corner the bolting man, they had split, and were chasing him from three different directions. The man came face-to-face with one of the cops, and the second one was converging at that very spot. However, the man escaped, simply running away from under their noses. The two gasping cops gave chase to the best of their sub-optimal abilities, but could not keep up with the runaway.

'It's not your fault,' Anant had told them. 'It's because of that,' he had said, pointing at their pot-bellies. After that incident, Anant had taken it upon himself to physically train his team and keep them *fighting fit*, in the literal sense. While the team had started reluctantly, they had soon realised the benefits and had gotten used to the daily fitness routine. Over the years, Anant had extended the regime to the entire ATS, so much so that clearing a rigorous annual fitness test was a non-negotiable condition to continue as a part of the squad.

'May I come in, sir?' Anant knocked at the office door of Navin Sarathi – the ATS chief and his boss. Anant knew something was amiss when Sarathi had called him that afternoon and asked him to investigate the murders in Netravathi Express. Ordinarily, this was a case for the crime branch, and not the ATS. Anant had gone directly from LTT to meet Sarathi.

'Come in,' Sarathi replied.

'Sir.' Anant saluted him.

'Have a seat.'

Over the next ten minutes, Anant briefed Sarathi on his observations. 'Sir, a question, if I may?' he asked at the end of his update. 'Sure,' Sarathi smiled. He knew what the question was.

'Why the ATS?'

'It all started yesterday,' Sarathi explained. 'We got information from RAW about a possible terror attack in Mumbai... let me be honest, we are *presuming* it will be an attack... the exact information we received was that arms were being delivered to Mumbai today... and how the arms-dealer would be traveling to Mumbai in the Netravathi Express... but we didn't know the name or identity... or any other details...' Sarathi paused. Anant nodded thoughtfully, rubbing his temple with his right index finger, as was his habit.

'So, the other man who got killed was...' Anant started.

'He was *our* man... undercover.' Sarathi and Anant were silent for a few moments. They both had lost team members to terrorism, time and again. But it wasn't a feeling one could ever get used to.

'So, what do we have on this woman?' Sarathi asked.

'Not much... the name in which her ticket was booked – Salma Abbas – is obviously fake. But I will still check it to be doubly sure. The attendant's description of her is not too helpful either... except that she had green eyes. I think she was wearing coloured lenses, so not much to go on.'

'Why do you think she was wearing lenses?'

'Sir, if she was trying not to attract attention, would she reveal anything about her that was so noticeable? I think it was to throw us off-track.'

'I agree. It seems very likely.'

'I have asked the team to check the CCTV footage at Thane. I will keep you posted.'

'Good. And what about the child? Obviously not hers,' Sarathi scoffed.

'Yes. I will follow up on that as well. Maybe we will get something there.'

'Great... anything else?'

'One more question, sir. How did RAW get the information?'

'Is that important?'

'Could be... not sure at the moment.'

'Hmm... let's figure it out,' Sarathi dialled a number on his mobile. 'Robin, my friend, how are you?' Sarathi said as Robin Dutta answered the phone. Anant leaned forward intently. Robin Dutta was one of the Joint Secretaries in RAW, functional head of the China and Southeast Asia desk. 'I am going to put you on speaker; Anant is here with me,' Sarathi said, as he kept the handphone on his desk and pressed the speaker button.

'Anant, how are you?' Robin's voice boomed in a heavy Bengali accent.

'Very well, sir... about the Netravathi Express incident... how did we get the lead?' Anant got straight to the point.

'We have a well-placed asset in the heart of the Chinese Politburo,' Robin replied.

'And?'

'Our asset passed on the information that a possible attack is being planned in Mumbai, and the travel details of the carrier. But could not tell us anything more.'

'Attack by China? Why?'

'*By* China or China *is in the know of it*. Both scenarios are likely. I wish our relations with the Chinese were better; it would have been simpler just picking up the phone and asking them if it was the latter!' Robin exclaimed.

'Hmm... anything else... likely target? When?'

'Nothing,' Robin sighed. 'Also, we do not know if the carrier was just an arms supplier or would be carrying out the operation himself.'

'Herself,' Anant corrected him.

'Pardon me?'

'We now know the operative is a woman,' Anant said, and gave a brief summary of the incident to Robin.

'Hmm... let me see if I can get my hands on any more information,' Robin said, and hung up.

'We may not have much time, Anant... smuggled arms don't remain unused for long,' Sarathi said.

Anant nodded in agreement, a grim look on his face.

13

M crossed the road, and hailed another auto-rickshaw. 'Sion station,' she said, and got in. The auto-driver, while surprised at having bagged such a long-distance fare, was visibly delighted. He switched on the music, and Bollywood chartbusters from the 1990s started competing with the din of the now increasing traffic. He looked in the rear-view mirror and smiled at his passenger, but she was staring out at the concrete landscape, with an expression he could not decipher.

M glanced at her watch. The bodies must have been discovered by now. And a hunt for the killer, *for her*, would be launched soon. How did the cop – the one who was imploring her to leave the cabin – come to know? Was he onto her? Or was it the other passenger he was after? She couldn't be sure. But a confrontation and examination of luggage would have blown her cover. The analysis didn't matter now, she concluded. They were both dead. And the boy was within a split second of being shot. She shook her head and smiled. Very few, if at all, were that lucky.

But this was exactly the kind of situation she wanted to avoid; she could have entered Mumbai simply enough, like millions of tourists. But 'he' had insisted on the subterfuge. *Nobody will ever suspect a woman carrying a small child, he had insisted.* She shook her head; she would not accept any interference in her planning henceforth.

Being an assassin was not easy, but over the years, she had learned to distance herself from her targets. Whenever she thought about them on a job, she pictured them as being already dead. It made things a lot simpler. And she believed it was good for them as well. It was a good way to die – quick and painless.

And of course, she loved the perks that came with the job.

Travel the world, see new places. She thought about her first trip to London. The first time she had worked with Lugovoy. At first, she had been disappointed when all she was asked to do was a recce of three hotels. She had given the details to Andrey in July 2006. After that, she did not hear anything from him for the next two months, until one day, towards the end of September, she received an envelope with '*For Medusa*' written on it. It contained a ticket to London for 16 October, and one metal diskette. The diskette fit snugly in the palm of her hand, and was no thicker than a wafer. She had to carry the silver diskette with her, and ensure she did not have too much exposure to it. She carried it simply enough, hidden in her make-up box, and nobody stopped her.

Andrey was on the same flight in business class; she saw him board after her. As agreed, they did not acknowledge each other. She could not contain her excitement, for she was sure something big was in the works, and she would have a role to play in whatever it was.

They hailed separate cabs from the airport and checked in within a few minutes of each other at the luxurious Millennium Hotel on Sloane Street, in Knightsbridge. She saw that Hyde Park was quite close to the hotel, and wondered if she would be able to go for a run during the trip.

A few minutes after she checked into her room, there was a knock at her door. It was Andrey.

'Give me the plate,' he told her, coming inside and closing the door behind him. She took out the metal diskette from inside her make-up kit and handed it over to Andrey. He slid it into a plastic bag and sealed it. He handed her a thin folder. 'Read it carefully,' he said, 'I'll see you at six at the reception.' He left as quickly as he had come. She saw the time – it was four in the afternoon.

She poured herself a glass of water, sat down at the study-table, and started reading the five-page document. On the first page, there was the photograph of a man she immediately recognized. *Alexander Litvinenko*.

Litvinenko was a former officer of the Russian Federal Security Service (FSB), one of the offshoot agencies formed after the KGB was dismantled. Andrey and Litvinenko had been peers in the KGB at one time. In the late 1990s, Litvinenko stirred up the proverbial hornet's nest in Russia after he accused the FSB, and the Russian president, of using terror tactics to frighten and subdue Russians. Discussions, money, threats – nothing worked. Litvinenko would just not stop, making one explosive accusation after another; but was shrewd enough to understand when he had crossed the point of no return. Before he could be arrested, he fled to the UK and sought political asylum, and had been staying there ever since. That was six years ago. From the UK, Litvinenko continued his tirade against the Russian establishment through media channels, but nobody knew where he was, until early 2006, when one of Andrey's operatives spotted him on Oxford street. Suddenly, the mission was clear to M.

They were in London to assassinate Alexander Litvinenko.

***

As she went through the dossier, she realized her recce to London earlier was the first step towards that goal. She had stayed at the Millennium for a day during that trip. The last page in the folder answered her curiosity about the silver, metal diskette she had carried with her. It was Polonium-210, or Po-210, as it was known as.

Po-210 was extremely toxic, she learned, and one microgram was enough to kill an adult. By weight, it is said to be 2,50,000 times more toxic that cyanide. And she had carried a Po-210 diskette in her make-up kit – she shuddered involuntarily.

The toxicity of Po-210 stemmed entirely from its radioactivity, and did not pose a threat outside of the body. It posed a fatal hazard only when ingested. Still, she decided to buy a new make-up kit. She closed the folder and kept it in her suitcase. She would shred it the moment she returned to Moscow.

Andrey was already waiting at the reception when she reached there at two minutes before six. Without exchanging a word, they walked out. There was a nip in the air, and M could see most people on the street in warm clothes. She felt comfortable enough though, and just had a light sweater on.

'Did you read the file?' Andrey asked her.

'Yes.'

'And?'

'When are we meeting Alexander?' M smiled mischievously at him.

It was half-past six when they reached Victoria Station. Andrey led her to Itsu, an Asian fast food and sushi restaurant. They sat down at a corner table, and pretended to be interested in the menu. Andrey kept surveying the entrance every few seconds. Sharp at seven, Litvinenko walked in, and spotting Andrey, waved to him. Andrey waved back with a big smile on his face. He stood up to meet Litvinenko and shook both his hands. He introduced M as his fiancée, Anna Kovtun. M smiled coyly at Litvinenko, playing the part of a blushing bride-to-be. Litvinenko was sporting a beard and had put on a little weight, but was easily recognizable from the photograph in the dossier.

They ordered food and drinks, and chatted away for almost two hours. Most of the discussions were about their KGB days and past colleagues. M participated intermittently, but was paying attention at all times. She observed how clever it was of Andrey to not allude to Litvinenko's criticism. She wondered what tricks Andrey had up his sleeves.

As the minutes passed, M felt herself getting more and more worked up. She had never felt this way before – this excitement was unlike any she had experienced. It was at that moment, having sushi at an Asian bar in London, that M realized that she was born for this – this was her purpose in life. In all of her missions, she would keep chasing this high.

'So, my friend,' Andrey said, becoming serious suddenly, 'it is time for you to come home.'

'Just like that?' Litvinenko asked.

'Yes, it is your country,' Andrey shrugged.

'And all is forgiven?'

'Absolutely. We start on a clean slate.'

Litvinenko fell silent. He sipped the beer, his fourth, and seemed to reflect on the proposal. Finally, he spoke, 'Hmm... will the president make a media announcement to that effect?'

'Media announcement?' Andrey looked surprised, and after giving it a thought, said, 'Yes, I can convince him on that.'

'I meant to the western media, not just the state-media?'

'I think I can manage that, too.'

'Ok... let me think about it,' Litvinenko said, and gestured to the server for the cheque.

'That's great,' Andrey said, and slid his hand inside his jacket. He took out a box of Cuban cigars and offered it to Litvinenko. 'For you, my friend. To a new beginning.'

M had read that Litvinenko loved to smoke, especially cigars. She had also read that Po-210 was most dangerous when inhaled from cigarette smoke. She was hoping he did not smoke one there. Litvinenko stared at Andrey for a moment, and then broke into laughter, 'My dear friend, I have given up smoking. It's been more than a year now.'

Andrey looked momentarily disappointed. Thankfully, Litvinenko did not notice it as his attention was diverted to the server who had come to their table with the bill. Andrey quickly recovered and said, 'That's good to know. You know, smoking kills.'

They both laughed. M joined in, wondering what they would do next.

Over the next two weeks, M noticed that Andrey was unusually pre-occupied. He often left the hotel in the morning, after breakfast – which they religiously had together – and returned late at night. M had instructions not to contact him, so all she could do was wait in her room. At best, she would sit in the hotel lobby for a couple of hours. She didn't risk going out, in case Andrey called her. But she was there for a purpose, and the endless waiting did not bother her in the least.

On 1 November, Andrey, for the first time since she had known him, arrived late for breakfast. Normally, he would always be there before her, at their usual table, sipping a piping hot Americano while reading the newspaper. She, at once, noticed he was not his usual calm and collected self. He let his coffee go cold, staring expectantly at his phone.

'Is everything okay?' she asked.

'Hmm... sorry, what was that?'

'Are you alright, Andrey?'

'Oh yeah... I am fine,' he said, sounding anything but.

Just then, his phone chimed Andrey grabbed it instantly and read the message. Almost immediately, his expression changed and he looked relieved. He grinned broadly at his protégé. 'Be ready, today is the day.'

It was almost 5 p.m. They were seated in the same coffee shop in the Millennium Hotel. Andrey seemed like his usual relaxed self. His light blue eyes twinkled as he sipped his regular coffee. At a minute past five, Litvinenko walked in through the main door of the hotel. Through the glass windows, M saw him make an enquiry at the reception, where the staff pointed him in the direction of the coffee shop. Litvinenko walked in, saw where they were seated, and joined them at the table. He did not look as enthusiastic as he did when she had last met him at Itsu.

'Hello, Alexander,' Andrey greeted him.

'Hello, Andrey,' Litvinenko said, as he shook his hand firmly.

'Hello, Anna,' he said as he smiled at M. She offered him her hand, and he gently shook it.

'So, how do we proceed? Things have not been very... positive... since we last met,' Andrey said slowly, coming straight to the point. He was referring to the fact that Litvinenko had, only two days after their meeting at Itsu, accused the FSB of murdering a Russian journalist, who was known for her critical reporting of the Russian state.

'Well, you tell me. I had to do the right thing,' Litvinenko replied.

'I understand. Nothing we cannot sort out. But first, some refreshments,' Andrey smiled, and waved to the staff. As if on cue, two servers came forward, with a tray of scones, cakes and a pot of tea.

'Thank you. And I will have a refill,' Andrey said, pointing to his cup. The servers nodded.

'Let me serve,' M said, politely dismissing the servers, as she poured tea into a china tea cup. 'Sugar? Milk?' she asked Litvinenko.

'One sugar, no milk. Thank you,' Litvinenko said, smiling at M.

M added sugar, stirred the tea carefully, and kept the spoon aside, far from her, towards Litvinenko's side plate. She slid the cup towards Litvinenko, who had bitten off a big chunk of a scone. He took a gulp of the liquid and smiled at M, raising his cup in appreciation. 'Just the way I like it.'

M fluttered her eyelids innocently and smiled at him, flashing her perfect set of teeth. She kept staring at Litvinenko, waiting for the Po-210 to take effect. She was expecting him to collapse as soon as he took a sip, but nothing of that sort happened. Litvinenko kept talking, and eating, as if nothing was wrong. He gulped down the tea, and then went for the pot again. M looked at Andrey, who avoided her gaze, and continued his discussion with Litvinenko, who was negotiating details about his return to Russia.

At six-thirty, Litvinenko bid adieu to Andrey and M, and left the hotel. M looked at Andrey, who shrugged and said, 'I don't know what happened.'

The mystery was solved two days later, when Litvinenko was taken to hospital after complaining of being violently sick. When Andrey and M heard the news, they left for Moscow on separate flights on the same day.

Litvinenko's condition worsened over the next few days, and he told the BBC he had been poisoned. The medical tests were inconclusive, and various reports started to emerge on the possible cause of his illness.

On 23 November, after he had signed a statement accusing the Russian president, Andrey Lugovoy and Anna Kovtun of poisoning him, Alexander Litvinenko died. He became the first known victim of induced acute radiation syndrome or radiation poisoning.

M experienced a thrill like never before. She had played a crucial part in history's first 'nuclear assassination'. And when she read Andrey's message to her – *Well done, Medusa* – she felt proud and powerful, like she could do anything. And get away with it.

***

'Madam... madam... where in Sion do you want to go?' The auto driver was asking her. Shaken out of her reverie, M looked at him, upset that he had interrupted her stroll down memory lane. They were at a junction; she could see the Sion railway station overbridge to her right.

'Here is fine,' she said, as the auto-rickshaw turned right. She stood at the crossing and looked around; while a lot looked familiar, the area was much more congested and noisier than she remembered. She was in the city after more than a decade. The street was packed with people – commuters walking to and from the station, shoppers crowding around hawkers and stalls that had encroached upon the already narrow road. She reached an old, two-storeyed grey building, its entrance hidden amongst the chain of stalls selling clothes. Just above the first level, a colourful signage announced – *Welcome International Inn, 3-Star, Second Floor.*

M needed to free her legs; she ignored the lift and climbed the two floors, stepping into a foyer that doubled up as the reception area of the hotel. The place smelled of cheap perfume. She walked up to the portly, middle-aged man at the counter, whose wrinkled face belied his heavily dyed black hair.

'One single room, please,' she said by way of greeting.

The man kept the magazine he was reading to the side, took off his reading glasses and looked up. He gave her a crooked smile as he looked her up and down. 'How many nights?'

'A month to start with.' She took out an envelope and handed over the cash. The man counted the cash, and slid across a printed form. 'Fill this, and show id proof,' he said curtly, without looking up.

M had read the reviews for the hotel, which were mostly poor. It was one of the main reasons she had chosen it; occupancy would be low. She scribbled a signature on the form without filling any other details. She then slid the form to the manager, along with another envelope, as thick as the one before. He did not bat an eyelid as he folded the envelope into the pocket of his trousers.

'Thank you,' M said as she took the key. Her room was at the end of the narrow corridor. She dumped her backpack on the bed and switched on the window air conditioner, that spluttered into action. She peeked outside the window, drawing the cheap curtains slightly. At the end of the road, she could see the bright yellow board of the Sion railway station.

14

NRanganathan, the newly appointed chairman of the board of Sethna Sons, one of India's most diversified conglomerates, was reviewing the final draft of the group's annual report, when the door to his plush cabin opened. 'He is almost here,' his secretary announced.

Ranganathan, or Ranga, as he liked to be called, kept the report in his drawer, got up and put on his dark-grey business jacket. As he walked towards his private elevator, he could not help but feel proud of the Sethna group's 150-year-old legacy. With more than a hundred operating companies and aggregate revenues of over 100 billion dollars, the Sethna group was synonymous with trust, not only in India, but across the world. Ranga, who had served the Sethna group for over thirty years in various capacities, was, for the last five years, on the board of the Sethna group until six months back, when he was elevated to the post of chairman of the board.

He smiled courteously at the employees who greeted him, acknowledging them by name, as he stepped out to the entrance of the group's iconic headquarters, a heritage building in south Mumbai known as The Bombay Quarters. Three of his company's top officials had also joined him. Almost immediately, a cavalcade of three cars pulled up at the entrance, led by a police car. Sanjay Adhikari got down from the first one, and with a warm smile, walked up to Ranga and hugged him.

'How are you, my friend?' Adhikari asked congenially.

'All good, Mr Future PM,' Ranga laughed.

'Too soon for that... there's many a slip... you know,' Adhikari sighed.

'You know you have all my support.'

'Thanks, I'll need it.'

Dalvi, who had accompanied Adhikari in the car, stood next to him, keenly inspecting the security arrangements. From the following car, two of the state's most promising politicians, Ajit Raut and Gautam Pawar, got down. They were Adhikari's closest aides, and carried a robust body of work behind them. Adhikari not only relied heavily on them for advice, but a lot of his accomplishments had been made possible due to the duo who executed his plans. The inseparable trio was a part of Maharashtra politics' folklore.

Over a year, the trio worked tirelessly on a vision to transform Mumbai into a futuristic megacity, which Adhikari branded as "Mumbai 2030". Once he thought he was ready, Adhikari presented it to the powers that were, including Doshi, when he was on a visit to the state. Impressed not only with Adhikari's passion, but also his planning, Doshi took him under his wings. And when the time came, Adhikari became the chief minister of the state. Adhikari never forgot his two allies in his rise to power, giving them formidable portfolios in the state.

Ranga exchanged pleasantries with Raut and Pawar, both of whom he had worked closely with in the past. He held them in high regard, and having seen his share of stubborn, corrupt politicians, was relieved the country was finally getting its share of young, passionate and educated politicians.

'Ranga, you are getting fitter by the day,' Adhikari remarked, walking alongside his friend of more than twenty years, as the group entered the building.

'Ah, I'm just trying my best,' laughed Ranga, who, at fifty-six, was lean and fit, thanks to his passion for long-distance marathon running.

Over the years, the Sethna group had sponsored several public initiatives, but the one closest to Ranga's heart had materialised just a few months ago – the Sethna group was now the sole sponsor of the annual Mumbai marathon. The group had been an associate sponsor of the mega-event since its inception a decade earlier; during which period the lead sponsor was a multinational bank. Due to mounting losses in its banking business, when the planning for this year's event was about to begin, the bank withdrew its sponsorship under pressure from its board. The bank's board did not see fiscal prudence to spend money on a 'mere sporting event' as they referred to it in their memo advising the withdrawal. It was an opportunity Ranga had been waiting for; he signed an exclusive agreement with the marathon's organizer, a US-based sports management company, to sponsor the event. The *'Sethna Mumbai Marathon'*, or *SMM* as it was re-branded. The first ever SMM was scheduled for 30 June, a little over two months away.

Ranga led Adhikari, Raut and Pawar to the board-room on the first floor of the building. As they settled into the comfortable chairs in the state-of-the-art meeting room, an attendant came in carrying a tray with bottles of mineral water. He noted down the beverage preferences of the guests and left the room as quietly as he had come.

'So, Ranga, how are the preparations coming along for the big event?' Adhikari asked, leaning forward with his hands on the rectangular teakwood table that could easily seat twenty people.

'It's quite good. I want to make it the biggest sporting event in Asia. I want to have the Mumbai marathon considered as one of the world majors in the next three years,' Ranga said, referring to the current six major marathons in the world. His excitement was palpable; Adhikari admired that about him.

'Why not? We will do it together... we will extend whatever support you need to make that happen,' Adhikari offered.

'It's on 30 June of this year, right?' Raut asked.

'Yes, that's correct. The last Sunday of June – that's when it is held every year.' Ranga smiled.

Just then, there was a soft knock at the door, and the attendant came in carrying another tray. Quietly, he served the guests their choice of beverage and kept a steaming mug of green tea in front of Ranga. He also kept two plates amongst the cups, one filled with an assortment of biscuits and the other, chocolates.

Raut helped himself to a piece of chocolate, and then another one, in quick succession. He was a slight man, almost skeletal, but had a bulging waistline that gave an odd shape to his build. His light-grey eyes twinkled with delight as he relished the expensive chocolates. Adhikari and Pawar helped themselves to a cream cracker each. Raut slid the plate of chocolates towards Ranga, who politely refused, and took a sip from his mug.

'Raut, you should certainly run the full marathon this year. You need to burn off all those chocolates,' Pawar joked, adjusting his silver-rimmed spectacles. Ranga and Adhikari joined in the laughter.

'Every man should be allowed one vice... this is mine,' Raut laughed, and devoured another large piece.

'Only god knows where all this goes,' Adhikari said, smiling and pointing to the chocolates, and then to Raut's frame.

'It all goes here,' Pawar continued the banter, pointing a finger towards Raut's protruding paunch.

'And here,' Raut added quickly, tapping his temple.

'That,' Adhikari jumped in, 'I completely agree. These two are my pillars of support.' The easy banter between Adhikari, Raut and Pawar was a result of hours spent huddled in boardrooms, discussing the city's and the state's endless problems and a relentless pursuit to make a real difference to people's lives. 'I don't know what I would have done without them.' He looked at Ranga.

Ranga nodded in agreement; he knew how the trio functioned as one well-oiled unit. Pawar bashfully looked at the floor, while Raut pursed his lips and stared ahead. It was a few seconds before Adhikari spoke, 'So Ranga, what is the route for this year's marathon? Has that been decided yet?'

'We intend to keep the route the same as every year. The full marathon and the *Dream Run* will start and end at CST, the half will start at Worli and end at CST.'

'Hmm... I had a different idea,' Adhikari started.

'Go ahead, I'll be happy to consider it,' Ranga replied, looking intently at Adhikari. He had always found Adhikari's suggestions to be sensible and took them seriously.

'Do you remember our discussion at Davos earlier this year?'

Ranga was a regular at the Davos summit. He was also a key advisory member of Doshi's *'Come to India'* initiative, that sought to invite global manufacturers and tourists to India under its catchy tagline. Introduced at the beginning of Doshi's first term, the program was a huge success, and had been a key factor in the improvement of India's ranking in all the global business indices. This year, too, Ranga was a part of a panel discussion at Davos, along with Doshi and a few other business stalwarts from India, for a session on India's emergence as a business super-power in the global economy.

During the summit, Ranga had caught up with Adhikari over a drink one evening, a session that had lasted until the wee hours of the next morning. Amongst many other things, the two friends had exchanged notes on the upcoming Mumbai marathon. Adhikari had also broken the news of Doshi's announcement to Ranga, who was more than thrilled to hear the news.

Ranga raised his eyebrows quizzically at Adhikari, and waited for him to continue.

'Like the Mumbai marathon is your dream project, my most ambitious project is also nearing fruition.'

'You mean... the....,' Ranga started. 'The Mumbai Coastal Road,' Adhikari interjected and completed the statement for him. He continued, 'The Coastal Road is almost ready. We're just carrying out some final checks.'

'So, what are you suggesting?' Ranga asked, leaning forward, his interest piqued.

Adhikari merely smiled at him, as he waited for him to catch up, with an expression that said – *Come on, I'm sure you can guess it.*

'Wait a minute... are you suggesting that for the Mumbai marathon... the route could be the Coastal Road?' Ranga exclaimed, visibly excited at the possibility.

'Yes! the Coastal Road,' Adhikari said, banging his hand on the table, a victorious smile on his face. He knew he had sealed the deal. 'In fact, let me make it even better. I want to inaugurate the Coastal Road with the Mumbai marathon. The marathon participants will be the first ones to experience the beauty of the Coastal Road.'

Ranga beamed with delight and leaned forward on the table, waiting for Adhikari to unfold the details of his plan.

***

'Let me make this more interesting,' Adhikari said, and nodded to Pawar. His trusted lieutenant unzipped his leather briefcase, and took out a plastic folder containing a sheaf of papers. Pawar unfolded a large map, and laid it out flat on the table in the conference room. As Ranga pushed the cups and trays away to make way for the chart, Raut grabbed two chocolates to munch on later.

'Here we are,' Adhikari said, thumping on the map of the city he loved. Ranga, Raut and Pawar were huddled around him. 'Let's get into the details of our plan,' he said, running his index finger along a bright red line on the map.

Almost a decade earlier, in the first year of the Doshi government, the idea of a sea-kissing highway alongside Mumbai's extensive coastline was conceptualized.

The first five years since the project's conceptualisation were spent, rather unproductively, in getting all the formal and legal approvals in place. Along the length of the Coastal Road was a combination of roads on stilts and roads built on reclaimed land. It also had two bridges and an under-sea tunnel.

It was to Adhikari's credit, that the complex construction of the Coastal Road was completed in a record time of four years. It was also a period when Raut and Pawar's executive and networking abilities were tested to the hilt, and they had helped Adhikari navigate through the pitfalls of ensuring construction was on time, citizens and activists were managed and the bureaucratic machinery chugged along nicely. To the utter amazement of the Mumbaikars, not a single case of corruption had tainted the Coastal Road project in all nine years, from its conceptualisation to almost completion.

After describing the Coastal Road's highlights, Adhikari paused and looked at Ranga, who was observing the route marked on the map carefully.

'Questions?'

'So, the full marathon is a distance of 42.2 kms; the half marathon is 21.1 and the Dream Run is 6... and the Coastal Road is 30 km one-way... so...,' Ranga thought aloud, drumming his fingers on the table.

Adhikari looked at Ranga, and then at the map. 'So, what are you thinking?' he asked.

'Tell me if this works. We flag off the race at Worli, and not at Nariman Point,' Ranga proposed.

'You want to bypass the first connector of 10 kms? Why?' Adhikari asked, perplexed.

'The Coastal Road covers a little over 20 kms one-way from Worli to Kandivali – so a return loop – *Worli-Kandivali-Worli* - works perfectly for the full marathon. The half-marathoners can turn here – at Versova – which is the 10-km mark,' Ranga said, pointing at the green dot on the map that said *Versova*, a popular western sea-side suburb. 'And the *Dream Run* participants,' Ranga continued, 'because they start much later, can turn at the 3-km mark on the Bandra-Worli sea-link itself. They will anyways have the entire bridge to themselves by then.'

Adhikari nodded silently, still poring over Ranga's suggestions on the route-map.

'Actually, it can work,' Raut added. 'The first stretch is only a connector. This route,' he continued, outlining the one proposed by Ranga, 'provides us with convenient return milestones. In fact, this will make it much easier to make arrangements.'

'I agree,' Pawar chipped in.

Adhikari looked up at Raut and Pawar, and then at Ranga. 'Let's go ahead with your suggestion.'

'That's fantastic. I'll let my team get started on the revised plans,' Ranga smiled.

'We'll make the announcement to the party, and get work started on the opening ceremony,' Adhikari told Raut and Pawar. 'I want the prime minister himself to inaugurate the Coastal Road.'

15

It was nearing 8 p.m. when Ashraf Siddiqui turned his bike to the left, under the JJ flyover, and made his way towards Bhendi Bazaar. The century-old area's name was a colloquial version of "behind the bazaar", a term used by the British to refer to the area behind Crawford Market. Bhendi Bazaar was also known as Bohri Mohalla, due to its large concentration of Dawoodi Bohra Muslims.

It was the month of Ramadan, and the streets were packed with people, famished after the daily ritual of fasting from sunrise to sunset. People had come out to honour *iftar*, the most important meal of the day during Ramadan. The tantalizing aroma of freshly roasted meat wafted through the air, with stalls selling delicacies to natives and tourists alike, who were out in equal numbers to enjoy the iftar feast.

Bhendi Bazaar, as an area, was developed in the *chawl* or dormitory fashion, specially designed to provide accommodation to single men who had moved to the city of dreams to earn a livelihood. Over time, their families also moved here, and forced closeness due to a lack of space gave birth to a distinct community culture. Lifelong friendships were forged over morning queues outside communal toilets and cutting chai shared in the lanes and by-lanes. Ashraf's grandfather, who worked as a construction labourer, was the first in their family to move here. His father ran a small hardware shop, which Ashraf had had no interest in. He had sold it a few months after his father died.

Ashraf could not wait to reach home. *Home*. He missed her, and wondered if he could have done anything differently. *Maybe. Maybe not.* He brushed the thought aside as he slowly but deftly navigated his bike through the sea of two-wheelers and people, many of them faces he had grown up seeing. His familiarity with his birth-place was diminishing fast, as the entire neighbourhood was on the cusp of a complete upheaval, and he struggled with the identity of the place. As a part of a massive redevelopment project led by the Saifee Burhani Upliftment Trust, Bhendi Bazaar was slated to get a facelift. Ashraf knew the place would look completely different in a few years, and wanted to soak in as much as he could of the disappearing neighbourhood while it still existed, scared that its unique culture would also get lost soon.

Ashraf parked his bike at the entrance of a crumbling four-storey building known as *Rahman Manzil*. Clutching his helmet in his right hand, he took the stairs, two steps at a time, to his one-room unit on the third floor. The doors of all the rooms were open what with people constantly moving in and out of each other's homes. He could not wait to see Naima.

On the third floor, he clicked open the lock to his room with a key. Switching on the lights and fan, he hung his helmet on a hook by the door. Ashraf smiled when he saw the photograph of Naima stuck on the wall. It was a recent photograph. His five-year-old was licking an ice-cream cone when Ashraf had clicked the picture at the Juhu beach. Her innocent, sparkling eyes conveyed pure joy. Ashraf rued the fact that he was not able to spend enough time with his daughter.

Keeping the door open, Ashraf turned left, crossed the staircase lobby and continued walking. Naima was at his childhood friend's house at the end of the corridor, where she stayed when he was at work. He dropped her off to school in the mornings, and *Ammi* – as she was known to everyone – his friend's old mother, picked her up at noon. Ashraf himself had spent most of his childhood at their home. The door was wide open, and Ashraf could smell *kebabs*. He smiled; he was starving. He abstained from food and liquids, including water, during the fasting period in Ramadan.

'*Abbu!*' Naima squealed with delight as she saw him, running towards him with her tiny hands outstretched. Ashraf lifted his daughter and kissed her greedily on the forehead. He sat down at the corner of the only bed in the room. An old lady, with tobacco-stained teeth, gave him a warm smile and got up, her legs creaking. 'I will get you some chai and kebabs,' she said.

'*Shukriya*, Ammi,' Ashraf smiled and said.

'Abbu, you had promised to take me out tonight,' Naima reminded him, sitting pretty on her father's lap.

'Yes, I remember. We will...,' Ashraf was interrupted by the standard ringtone of his mobile phone. He answered at the second ring.

As always, Ashraf listened attentively to the voice at the other end. 'I'll be there in fifteen minutes,' he said finally and hung up.

Ashraf saw Naima's expectant eyes, and immediately turned away. He gently laid his daughter down on the bed, caressed her head, and said softly, 'Abbu has to go for some very important work. We will go out tomorrow, okay?'

The little girl nodded; her eyes moist with disappointment. Ashraf quietly turned around and left the room. The old lady kept the cup of tea and the plate of kebabs on the floor; she hugged Naima and tickled her. The little girl laughed, but her eyes followed the retreating figure of her father.

Ashraf, on his way down, picked up his helmet and locked the door to his room. He kickstarted his bike and slowly made his way out of the festive bazaar.

16

A nant Kulkarni was a worried man. The CCTV footage at Thane station turned out to be a dead end. The woman in the burqa had hailed an auto-rickshaw outside the station. The Thane police had identified the auto-rickshaw from its registration number plate and questioned the driver, who recollected the passenger as she had boarded the vehicle saying she wanted to go to Viviana mall, but had gotten down way before reaching the mall. She got down soon after speaking to someone on the phone – maybe a boyfriend or lover, the driver said.

Does she have an accomplice? Lost in thought, he was fidgeting with the paper-weight on his desk, when he heard a knock at his door.

'Ah, you're here, come in,' he said, on seeing the familiar face.

Sub-inspector Ashraf Siddiqui saluted his boss and mentor, and stood in attention.

'Take a seat, Ashraf,' Anant said, pointing to the chair opposite his.

'Thank you, sir.'

Anant smiled. That was one thing he admired about Ashraf; they had worked together for many years, on many cases, but he never took advantage of the familiarity. He had never sought any favours, or demanded a promotion or salary hike. *Hell, he had never taken leave,* Anant thought. *Except that one heart-breaking time two years back.*

'We have a situation, Ashraf.'

'Sir,' Ashraf leaned forward.

'Before I start, have you broken your fast?'

'Not yet, sir. But that can wait.'

Anant waved off the suggestion and dialled '9' on his desk-phone. 'Get a mutton biryani in my cabin,' he ordered at the office cafeteria, and hung up.

'That wasn't necessary, sir,' Ashraf said, in his usual reticent manner. Anant just smiled and nodded.

Anant brought Ashraf up-to-speed on the case. Ashraf soaked in all the details, interjecting with a question from time to time. There was a knock at the door, and Anant waved in a young office boy, who brought in the biryani on a plastic plate, with a spoon and a bottle of water. Ashraf ignored it, and focused all his attention on the brief his boss was giving.

'I hope you're up for a challenge,' Anant asked, sliding the plate towards Ashraf. Ashraf offered a silent prayer and dug into his dinner. He knew Anant would eat later, so he didn't offer him any.

Ashraf just smiled. 'What's next?' he asked.

'We have two things that we can start with,' Anant said. 'One, the child from the train. I went to the hospital today. He is still unconscious; maybe due to the effects of the heavy drugs... let's hope he recovers soon and we can get an idea as to what happened.'

'And the other?'

'We just have to find *one* woman in this city of *two crore* people. Simple.'

'Looks like we have our work cut out for us.'

17

Chen Jintao was sweaty, despite the cold weather. He was filled with two strong emotions – anger and dread – as he paced up and down the verandah of his sprawling mansion in Chaoyang, the richest district in Beijing.

He was not looking forward to the phone call. *A shootout in the train? How did that happen?* The peaceful quiet was broken by the shrill ringing of Jintao's private number. Only one person had that number; and he called only that person from the number, which, they had ensured, could not be traced to either of them.

'Yes, I heard,' Jintao said, as he answered the phone, pre-empting the obvious.

'Not the start we were hoping for,' said the voice at the other end.

'But no damage is done... we are still on track with the plan.'

'On the contrary, from a position of zero risk, there is now a serious threat to the plan. The ATS is pursuing the case. How could this happen?'

Jintao stayed silent. He knew he was caught on the wrong foot, and he knew what he had to do next. 'I will find out how it was leaked out,' he offered defensively.

'Yes, do that. We do not want another mishap. And I don't have to tell you – don't trust *anyone*.'

'Of course,' Jintao said.

'On a brighter note, I have finalised the date.'

'That's great. When is it?'

For the next ten minutes, the Serpent explained to Jintao what he had in mind. 'Well, what do you think?' he asked the Chinese foreign minister when he was done.

'Brilliant.... Khorgos awaits you.' Jintao smiled for the first time that day. But he still had to find the traitor in his midst.

18

Ten days had passed since M's arrival in Mumbai. Other than a brief outing every morning, when she would walk till the end of the hotel block to pick up the daily newspaper and have her flask of tea replenished from a local *tapri*, she had hardly stepped out of her hotel room. Only on one other occasion, she had gone out to buy some clothes from a nearby garment shop. She had all her meals in the room; she would pick up some breakfast on her way from the newspaper stall. At times, she would take away lunch too at the same time. For all other meals, she would order from one of two nearby restaurants, calling them directly from the in-room landline phone. She always kept cash with the receptionist, who would accept the food delivery and let her know when it arrived.

She was waiting for her next instructions. The one thing she had in abundance was patience. It was an acquired trait, from her days of training with the Spetsnaz, the Russian special forces. The Spetsnaz training was similar to that of the British SAS or the U.S. Navy Seals, aimed at making the Russian special forces experts in the fields of covert operations, assassinations and reconnaissance. She had excelled in long-distance marksmanship, and as a sniper, could lie waiting in the same position for hours, motionless, without losing her focus for a second. Compared to that, this assignment felt almost like she was on vacation. *So far, at least.*

***

Her most cherished memory from the training days was when Andrey coached her personally over a week. At the end of the Spetsnaz training, the one or two exceptional candidates from

71

every batch were selected for individual coaching. That year, it was only M.

On the first day of the coaching, Andrey picked her up in his Lada Largus. M saw that Andrey was alone, without a driver; she blushed as she sat in the car. They exited Moscow and drove for around two hours, passing by lush green forests, ancient towns with picturesque churches and pre-historic nineteenth century houses. Andrey slowed down along the banks of the Istra river, and just when M thought they had reached a dead end, Andrey took a turn on to a country road, almost completely hidden from sight. After a bumpy ride for twenty minutes, the path widened and within a kilometre, they were at the gates of a large estate. A red-bricked chalet, blemished but beautiful, stood at the centre of the estate, surrounded by fields and trees.

'Come on in,' Andrey said, as he led her inside the single-storeyed cottage. M was taken aback; it was just one large hall that comprised most of the interior, and a closed room at one end. M walked over to a glass showcase, the only other furniture in the room other than two large sofas and a centre-table. M slowly walked along the showcase; on display in the shelves were varieties of thermos flasks, mess tins, motor oil cans, watches and pens. She turned around; a questioning look on her face.

Andrey smiled; he was expecting this reaction from her. 'During World War II,' he explained, 'the Nazis had some very creative ideas about how to sneakily attack British ships and British leaders. They designed bombs looking like everyday items, and used them frequently, although not too effectively, in my opinion.'

With a renewed interest, M bent forward to study the contents of the showcase. 'May I touch them?' she asked.

'Sure, they have been deactivated, don't worry,' Andrey laughed.

'Wow!' M exclaimed; she was mesmerized as she held each item, amazed by the detailing of every piece. She was certain not even trained eyes would be able tell that those were bombs.

'Let me show you how they are detonated,' Andrey offered, 'and importantly, teach you how to make them.'

'Really?' M screamed, like an excited child.

'Yes, that's what the coaching week is for,' Andrey smiled at her and pointed to the closed room, which she then realized was a workshop. But she could not help feel a tad disappointed that a week alone with Andrey would not be spent on anything more interesting. She started walking towards the room.

'Before we start,' Andrey called out, 'I want you to see this one – it's my favourite.'

'This is...a bomb?' M stood riveted; her eyes transfixed on the object Andrey was holding in his hand.

'It most definitely is. Winston Churchill escaped it; I am sure your target won't.'

***

She missed Andrey, not only for professional reasons. He was the only man she was drawn towards; his power, his calm control over every situation and his sheer magnetism. A heady combination that she found irresistible. She had always imagined a future with him. For a moment, she looked at her mobile phone lying by the bedside. She had not spoken with him for years. *Should I call?*

She quickly brushed the thought aside and poured herself a cup of tea from the thermos. She sat down on the only chair in her room, and picked up *The Sunday Times of India*. It was her second Sunday in Mumbai. She quickly turned to the matrimonial section in the classifieds, and scanned through the *Brides Wanted* columns. Her eyes lit up when she saw the advertisement she had been waiting for.

Alliance invited for educated businessman, having coastal properties in Beijing and Russia. Age 30, 6-feet tall. In Mumbai for an event only for today. Contact between 2 - 4 p.m. on 961394183.

She fetched her diary and pen to make notes, and scanned through the message carefully. *Beijing and Russia* were the keywords to look for in the matrimonial section, along with a truncated mobile number at the end – nine digits instead of ten. For each of the digits, she started writing a new number on her note-pad. For the first digit, one number lower than the number in the advert; for the second, one higher; and so on alternately. She added a '1' at the end; the last additional digit always remained the same in the code. She memorised the complete number – *8704850921* – and tore up the piece of paper. She would dispose it off when she went out next. She glanced at her watch; it was still a few hours before she could make the phone call.

She studied the message again. It reconfirmed the location was Mumbai. Now, she also had a date – from the age and height description. 30 June. *What else was in there?* After a few minutes, her eyes lit up when she got the answer she was looking for. There was an additional clue in the advertisement – *coastal*. She got up and picked up the previous Tuesday's edition from a neatly arranged stack of newspapers in the corner. She flipped the paper to page four and was greeted by a beaming Sanjay Adhikari, the chief minister of Maharashtra, and N Ranganathan, the chairman of Sethna Sons. The two men were posing for the press in front of the famous Bombay Quarters building, their fists raised high in victory.

The wait is over - Mumbai Coastal Road to be inaugurated with the Sethna Mumbai Marathon on 30 June, announced the headlines. She read the article carefully.

Well, the wait was certainly over, she thought. She closed her eyes, forming an outline of how she would execute her mission.

19

Anant headed towards his cabin after a status update meeting with Sarathi, when his phone buzzed. It was one of his leads on the train shootout case. 'Seb, have you got something?' he asked.

An old friend of Anant's, Sebastian Rego was the station-in-charge at the Panjim police station in Goa. Before joining the ATS, Anant had helped Rego crack a high-profile rape-and-murder case. The body of a twenty-five-year-old British tourist had been washed ashore outside a famous beach club in Goa. It was Rego's first big case, and Anant had helped him with the Mumbai leg of the investigation, along with a few useful tips on how to proceed with the probe. The case, which had threatened to escalate into a major diplomatic stand-off between the two countries, was solved in quick time. It was Rego's claim to fame, and the two had kept in touch ever since.

After the train shootout, Anant had sent a picture of the little boy to Rego. 'The suspect boarded the train from Goa with this boy. See if you can get anything on him,' he had asked Rego.

Seb had called Anant to update him. 'The boy went missing around ten days back. A complaint was registered with the Madgaon police station, and investigations were ongoing, when I received the boy's picture from you,' Rego replied.

'How did the boy disappear?'

'Well, I just got the call from the Madgaon station, so we'll get the details when I meet them. What's this all about?'

'I am coming there in person... I would like to get my hands on some details myself. I'll brief you all about it when I get there,' Anant replied.

'Sure, it will be great to see you again, Anant.'

'Likewise, Seb.' Anant hung up, and called Ashraf to his cabin. 'Finally, we may get the break we are looking for,' he told him as he sat down. 'Speak to Shinde and book us for the first flight out to Goa tomorrow morning.'

'Yes, sir,' Ashraf said, and dialled Shinde, the administrative in-charge at the ATS.

Anant's phone rang again; he picked it up the moment he saw *Home* flashing on the screen. He spoke on the phone for a few seconds before dashing out of his cabin, with Ashraf in tow.

***

Hindu colony is an old locality situated in the central Mumbai area of Dadar. Although traditionally Maharashtrian, the area is fairly cosmopolitan now. Rampant redevelopment had lent a completely new look to the area; but some parts were still frozen in time, with a few buildings still retaining their original design of the pre-independence era. The peaceful quiet of the neighbourhood was broken by the screeching of tyres, as Ashraf parked the police car inside the compound of a two-storeyed apartment in lane number 5 of the colony.

Anant jumped out of the police car before it came to a complete halt, and rushed inside the building. He ran up the two floors to his flat; the door was opened before he could ring the bell. 'How is she, Suchita?' he asked the young, slight girl as he entered. Without waiting for an answer, he rushed into the bedroom. The woman on the bed was fast asleep, her heart beating softly against her yellow cotton dress. A pale version of her earlier self, she still looked very beautiful. Her once long tresses were short now, barely grazing her delicate shoulders.

Suchita had followed Anant into the bedroom, and was standing quietly beside him. 'What happened?' Anant asked her, almost in a whisper.

'Hey,' the sleeping woman stirred, 'you're back?'

'Nandini, are you okay? Did you take your medicines?' Anant asked his wife of fourteen years.

'I am fine... why did you rush home? She panics unnecessarily,' Nandini said, smiling gently at Suchita. With an effort, she sat up, and leaned against the headrest of the bed. Anant sat down next to her, and slid a pillow behind her.

'How are you, *apa*?' Ashraf knocked at the open door of the bedroom, and peeped in. He knew Nandini well, and regarded her as his elder sister, or apa.

'Ashraf... good to see you. How is Naima?' Nandini smiled at him. She was very fond of the little girl, who was a frequent visitor at the Kulkarni's.

'She is fine, apa,' Ashraf said, and then looking at Anant, 'Can I get something, sir?'

'No, no... sit down... let's have some chai,' Nandini said, and got down from the bed.

Anant held her, and walked with her to the living room, where they all settled down. Suchita, on cue, went into the kitchen, and came out with two glasses of water, which she kept on the centre-table. Anant forced Nandini to have a sip from his glass. She protested at first, but finally gave in.

Ashraf smiled sadly. The last few years had been tough on the Kulkarnis, he reflected, gazing into his glass of water. First, the accident; and then, just when Anant and Nandini had started recovering from the trauma, a regular health check-up the previous year had thrown their lives out of control. The doctor had insisted on a follow-up test, after which Nandini was diagnosed with blood cancer. *Advanced stage.* Initially overwhelmed, Nandini had come to terms with reality in a few months; but Anant was still in denial. He was angry as well, though he tried not to let it show. *There were no warning signs. How could she get it? She doesn't smoke, doesn't drink... how could this happen?* He had taken Nandini to the best doctors in the city, hoping for a different diagnosis. Like a child, he was seeking a different answer to the same question. His thoughts were interrupted when his mobile buzzed.

'Yes, Shinde,' Ashraf said, as he picked up the call. 'Email me the tickets, but I don't think sir would be coming now.'

Anant shook his head. Nandini looked at him questioningly. 'Following up on a case. It's nothing serious. Ashraf will manage it,' he told her.

'Anant, I am perfectly fine. You cannot cancel your plans on my account... don't worry... I will keep you updated of my wellbeing every hour.'

Anant sighed and looked at her hesitatingly. It was a constant conflict he was trying to resolve in his head. Although he almost always pushed the thought away, his rational mind told him he may not have much time left with Nandini. He had come very close to submitting his resignation a few times, but Nandini had held him back from doing so.

20

M slowly walked along the Worli sea-face. It was a Sunday evening and the neighbourhood was crowded with people. The man she had called had chosen the place well. An extremely popular weekend spot, the promenade alongside the sea, popularly known as the *Millionaire's Mile*, was barricaded, with the crowds crammed on the opposite side, alongside the homes of Mumbai's upper-class. A few evening walkers and joggers, used to the hordes, skillfully navigated their way through them.

A few young bikers had parked their bikes next to the fence that cordoned off the road. Two of them had climbed atop their two-wheelers to get a glimpse of the new promenade on the other side of the temporary wall, which was not yet open to the public. *Mumbai Coastal Road Project – Connecting People and Places* was stamped across the barriers in bright yellow paint against a blue background.

The construction of the Coastal Road along this stretch of land had faced its fair share of problems. The previous two-kilometre long, eighty-five-year-old promenade extended from the INS Trata at its northern end to the Worli Dairy at its southern. The residents had staged multiple protests to save the walkway as the municipal corporation of Mumbai, or the BMC, had started working on the ambitious project. They were fearful of losing not only a much-cherished promenade, but also the area's charm and history. The residents had backed down only after the chief minister, Sanjay Adhikari, had personally intervened and promised a better, swankier sea-side walkway. This new walkway, now ready, was four-kilometres long, with a large green patch separating the existing sea-facing road and the Coastal Road. The residents across the street could see the development from their balconies and terraces, and were looking forward to the inauguration of the new promenade on the day of the Sethna Marathon.

M reached the statue of R.K. Laxman's *Common Man*. She had been informed of the meeting place by the man she spoke with on the number derived from the newspaper advertisement. She glanced at her watch – it was about time. She did not have to wait long as at the stroke of six, a thin man of average height, wearing a light blue *I Love Mumbai* t-shirt, crossed the busy junction and walked over to the statue. He waited there, carrying a copy of *The Sunday Times of India* in his hands. M, who was lingering nearby, went across to him. 'Do they have such roads in Beijing?' she asked.

The man was clearly taken aback, though only for a split second, when he saw the plain looking, salwar-kameez clad woman in front of him. She could have been any middle-class woman from the six million women who lived in the city. His sharp eyes scanned M from top to bottom as he ran his fingers through his short, salt-and-pepper hair. M noticed that his pointed goatee and moustache were speckled with more salt than pepper.

'Let's go,' he said by way of greeting. M followed him across the road, where he led her to a white Maruti Wagon-R, possibly amongst the most common cars in the city. 'Bandhu Yadav,' he said, as he sat down in the driver's seat and extended his hand.

'M', she replied, shaking his hand firmly.

Bandhu looked at M expectantly, waiting for her to say something more. 'That's it – *M*?' he asked after a few seconds.

'Yes, that's it,' M said, matter-of-factly. 'Shall we go?'

Bandhu shrugged and put the car in gear. As they neared the junction, a traffic constable whistled loudly and stopped all cars coming towards the sea-face. Soon, a few other cops also arrived at the intersection. Within a few minutes, cars had lined up on both sides of the traffic lights at the junction; a few of them started honking, till the cops knocked on their windows.

Police sirens broke the silence of the evening as a cavalcade made its way towards the sea-face. Three police cars escorted two SUVs, as onlookers lined the street.

'It's the chief minister,' M overheard a cop telling an inquisitive driver. She got down from the car, and walked towards the main road, where the convoy had stopped. Sanjay Adhikari got down from his SUV, waved to the crowd that had gathered, and walked to the barricaded connector to the Coastal Road. His entourage surrounded him from all sides. As he made his way through the makeshift gate on to the Coastal Road, M got her first look at the man she was assigned to kill.

***

'Be back in ten,' M told Bandhu as he stopped the car near Sion station.

'Okay, I'll be in that lane,' Bandhu said, pointing to an adjacent street. M nodded and headed to the Welcome International Inn. It was dark by the time they had reached Sion, and the signage was backlit in neon. Thankfully, the reception desk was unmanned. M packed her bag quickly and inspected the room carefully to make sure she hadn't left anything behind before leaving the hotel.

She walked over to the waiting car and dumped her bag in the backseat. Bandhu took a U-turn at Sion circle, and drove towards Wadala. He crossed over a railway overbridge eastwards as he entered the congested central suburb. Right at the end of the bridge, he took a sharp left turn into a narrow, almost deserted lane. The harbour line of the Mumbai railways ran on one side of the road, while a few stray slums and a vacant warehouse occupied the almost barren stretch on the other. At the end of the road stood a residential tower – Centrum Residency – that looked completely out of place in its surroundings. Bandhu drove the car into the almost-empty parking lot of the twenty-storeyed building.

'Most of the apartments are unoccupied,' Bandhu explained, looking at M. 'It was leased by a company to offer serviced apartments to its employees, but the company went bust and the real estate in the area never took off.'

M looked around her as they walked towards the elevators, carefully checking out exits and entries in case of contingencies. An old security guard sitting at the entrance of the elevator lobby was engrossed in his mobile phone, and did not look up. Bandhu pushed 18th button in the elevator. There were four units on their floor; they entered 1803, a three-bedroom flat, sparsely furnished. M put her bag into one of the bedrooms, that overlooked the railway tracks. *An apartment here wouldn't have cost a lot,* M thought. *Not that money mattered to the man who had paid for it.*

She took a long, hot shower, thinking over her plans for the next few days. And Bandhu. She would have to get rid of him at the end of the mission. The man she knew only as the Serpent had readily agreed to that. *No loose ends,* he had said. She wondered if he had planned a similar fate for her. But she was prepared for that. As she changed and stepped out into the living area, which was just a hall with two black sofas and a television, she realized she was famished. Bandhu was sprawled on one of the sofas, watching the news on the TV. Just then, the doorbell rang. Bandhu sprang up and opened the door, without checking through the peephole. M frowned.

'There you are,' Bandhu said, as he opened the door to a plump man with greasy, curly hair. He was carrying a plastic bag in one hand and a thick, sealed envelope in the other. He handed over the plastic bag to Bandhu as soon as he entered the flat. He raised his thick, bushy eyebrows when he saw M. She was amused when she saw the boyish-looking, bespectacled man the

Serpent had told her about in advance. *He is a fixer; will get you anything you want in Mumbai,* he had said. M realized that he was almost the same height as Bandhu, but appeared shorter due to his bulky frame.

'This is Tamas,' Bandhu said, 'and this is M,' he said, making introductions with his hands, as he went into the kitchen with the plastic bag. Tamas smiled at M, who nodded in reply. 'This is for you,' Tamas said, handing over the envelope to M. She carefully removed the seal, and took out the contents on one of the sofas. Two handsets and at least a dozen SIM cards. All prepaid, bought under fake identities. There was another smaller, sealed envelope inside the larger one, which she kept for later.

Bandhu came out with a few plates, and opened the food packets that Tamas had brought with him. The trio settled down on the cool floor, and dug into the *pulao,* eating in silence for the next ten minutes.

After dinner, M retired to her room, while Bandhu and Tamas sat in the hall, watching TV and chatting. They had obviously worked together before, M observed. She locked the door to her room from the inside and opened the other envelope. It contained four fake identity documents she could use. She looked at the altered images of herself in them; each one quite unlike the others. She could easily manage that bit, she smiled, as she turned her attention to the two sheets of paper. As she went through the detailed itineraries and schedules, she felt a sudden rush of adrenaline. *It certainly helped to have someone on the inside. She knew that. She had been one when at the embassy.*

21

Anant smiled at the little girl, and raised his hand to offer her a high-five. The three-year old giggled, and ran away to her mother, who was sitting on the adjacent sofa. Anant looked at the young expectant mother, who was immersed in a magazine. She must have been around seven months along, Anant reckoned. He looked around the brightly coloured reception room with pictures of smiling, playing babies on the walls. There was one more pregnant woman waiting, her baby bump barely visible. She was accompanied by an older woman, most likely her mother, going by their striking resemblance.

The little girl was now playing with a soft toy, chatting animatedly with the blue elephant. Anant glanced at the time on his mobile phone – it was almost 5 p.m., and he guessed they would be in next. He had planned to pick up Nandini on his way to the doctor, but due to a last-minute change in plans, he had to be on the other side of town. So, they had decided to meet directly at the clinic. Anant liked to be before time for any of his appointments while Nandini was a last-minute kind of person. He had called her when he was almost at the clinic; she had just started from home. In spite of his insistence that she should take a cab, she was driving herself to the clinic. I should have picked her up, Anant told himself.

He tapped his right foot on the ground impatiently. He called Nandini's number; but she did not pick up. Just then, the door to the doctor's consulting room opened and a beaming young woman walked out. 'Mrs Sharma, please come in,' a pleasant looking receptionist called out. The woman next to Anant placed the magazine on the centre-table and slowly got up and went inside. It would be their turn next, Anant knew. He called Nandini again, but there was no answer.

Anant pressed her number again. After what seemed like an eternity, she answered the call. 'Anant, I am on my way, please don't...' The rest of her words were drowned in a sea of sounds – blaring honks, tyres screeching and metal exploding.

'Nandini? Nandini, are you there? Nandini...' Anant screamed.

***

Anant was jolted awake as the aircraft touched down noisily. He was drenched in sweat – his shirt stuck to his back and neck despite the air conditioning – with both his hands clutching the arm-rest tightly. The stewardess announced their on-time arrival at the Dabolim International Airport in Goa and Anant unfastened the seat-belt as the nightmare replayed in his head. *What if I had not called her? What if I had picked her up? My daughter would have been five years old.* In his mind, the baby was always a daughter. He sighed and took a sip of tepid water from a bottle kept in the seat-pocket.

As Anant and Ashraf walked out of the arrivals terminal, they spotted Rego. They shook hands and climbed into the police car, Rego taking the wheels. The tall, sturdy Goan cop was wearing his trademark Ray-Ban Aviators. He was never seen without his sunglasses and Anant wondered if he also slept with them on.

'So, where are we on the missing boy's case?' Anant asked Rego, once they had caught up.

'The boy stayed at a shelter for children called Baby Steps in Madgaon. It helps almost a hundred kids up to the age of ten. Around half of them are orphans, or do not know the whereabouts of their parents; these kids stay full-time at the shelter. The rest of the children – their parents are mostly day labourers and the kids are provided meals and basic schooling at the shelter. These kids return home in the evening.'

'And our boy?'

'Ryan. Parents not known... Has been living at the shelter since he was abandoned at its door when he was just two days old. He went missing around ten days back. How is he doing now, by the way?'

'He is still under observation, the poor kid. Once he recovers, we will arrange for his return,' Anant explained. 'Are we headed directly to the shelter?'

'Yes, it's in Madgaon, on old station road...very close to the railway station. We should be there in about half an hour.'

The traffic was lighter than usual, and they reached the shelter in under thirty minutes. Baby Steps was a single-storeyed building, diagonally opposite a chapel. There was a small public playground directly behind the building. On seeing the police car, the security guard in a blue-grey uniform opened the gates and pointed to a parking space in the compound of the shelter.

Rego knocked on the glass door of a cramped room that served as the office, and without waiting for the old woman sitting inside to respond, walked in. Anant and Ashraf followed him in. The heavy-set woman looked at the three men through her thick glasses, clearly surprised. She was about to say something when Rego showed her his police ID. She gestured to the two chairs opposite her desk, and looked awkwardly at the cops; there was no room for a third chair.

Rego and Anant sat down; Ashraf waved calmly to the lady, as if telling her not to worry about it. He stood on one side, leaning lightly on the thin, laminated wall.

'How can I help you, Inspector?' the lady asked in a hoarse voice.

'You can start by telling us more about Ryan's disappearance, Mrs D'sa,' Anant said, having read the name-plate on the desk.

The woman leaned forward, resting her elbows on the side-arms of her chair, that squeaked at the movement. She remained motionless, quietly looking at the policemen.

'How did the boy disappear?' Anant prompted.

'He was playing in the ground with the other kids... in the evening... but did not return with them. 6 p.m. is when the bell rings and they have to be back by then,' Mrs D'sa explained.

'And when did you realize he was missing?'

'Within an hour, at most... when the children gathered for their evening meal. We looked around for him... in the grounds, the common classroom and the dormitory.... but he was nowhere to be found.'

'I see. And when did you lodge a police complaint?'

'The next morning...we searched for him all night...and thought he would return in the night.'

Anant nodded, not entirely convinced. 'You said we searched for him. Who all are you referring to?'

'Oh... just the staff and the other children.'

'I would like to meet the staff please.'

'We don't have a big team, as you can understand. It's just me, two staff and two security guards. The guards work in shifts.'

'I understand.... Can we speak to them?'

'Sure, please follow me.'

Mrs D'sa got up with a grunt and started to walk out of the room. Anant saw a framed photograph hanging on the wall and stopped to get a closer look. It was a celebration of sorts; around two dozen children with Mrs D'sa and a thin, balding man next to her.

'That was last Christmas,' Mrs D'sa said, when she saw Anant looking at the picture.

'And who is this?' Anant asked, tapping on the man's picture.

'That's Omkar, my assistant. He helps with everything – office-work, groceries. He also takes care of the children when they play outside.'

'Let's speak with Omkar in that case,' Anant said.

'He hasn't come to work for the last few days. Called in sick.'

'Can you give me his phone number?'

'Sure,' Mrs D'sa picked up a handset lying on her table, and bringing it close to her thick spectacles, punched in some keys. Then she handed it over to Anant, showing him the screen. Anant noted down Omkar's number and dialled him from his phone. The number was unreachable.

He clicked a picture of the framed photograph and the group left the office, following Mrs D'sa. She led them into an open area next to the office, which appeared to be the dining area. A few kids were playing there; they stopped to look at the visitors briefly, but soon resumed their activity. A thin woman in a worn-out saree was sitting on the floor at one end of the room. She was mashing potatoes in a large vessel. 'This is our cook,' Mrs D'sa said, pointing at her.

The saree-clad lady stood up as she saw the group approaching her. She appeared frightened, and looked at her boss with wide, surprised eyes.

'Don't worry, we just want some information about the day Ryan went missing,' Anant said in an assuring tone, sensing her unease.

'I looked everywhere, sir... the dormitory... bathrooms... but couldn't find him anywhere...I don't know anything else, sir.'

'And the playground? Ryan was playing there before he went missing, right?'

'I am not sure, sir... Omkar looked for him outside.'

***

'Thank you for your help. In case you remember something that might help us, please call me,' Anant told Mrs D'sa, after doing a round of the premises. He saved his contact on Mrs D'sa's phone before leaving. He showed her his name and number. She nodded.

'When will Ryan come back?' she asked.

'Very soon.'

As the group walked towards the car, they saw the security guard looking nervously at them. Anant glanced behind to see Mrs D'sa staring after them. They sat in the car and drove off.

Mrs D'sa walked back to her office and dialled a number. 'The police were here... the boy could be a problem for us,' she said, when the call was answered.

'I will take care of it,' said the person at the other end.

***

It was almost 3 p.m. by the time they left the shelter. 'I don't know about you guys, but I am starving,' Rego announced. 'Let me treat you to a nice Goan fish curry.'

'Works for me,' Anant said, giving him a thumbs-up sign.

'Ashraf *miyaan*, you are fine with that?' Rego asked, looking at Ashraf in the rear-view mirror.

'Last few days of Ramadan,' Ashraf said, smiling at Rego.

'Damn, what a pity, man!' Rego said, slamming his palms on the steering wheel.

As they waited for their order to be served at a famous shack Rego took them to, Anant called up Nandini to check on her. He was relieved to know that she was feeling fine; she sounded better too. As Rego and Ashraf chatted away, Anant dug quietly into the fish-curry and rice. Anant was a tad disappointed by their visit so far. He had hoped they'd find a solid lead in Goa, but that had not happened. Yet, he felt he was onto something.

'So, when is the flight back?' Rego asked, looking at Ashraf.

'First flight out tomorrow morning,' Ashraf replied.

'Hmm... not a very useful trip, huh?' Rego said. Ashraf only shrugged.

'There is just one more thing I want to check on first,' Anant said, looking at his two colleagues.

***

'May I know what are we waiting for?' Rego asked, looking impatiently at Anant. It was almost 9 p.m., and they had spent the past two hours sitting in the police car, parked around a hundred metres away from the shelter. Ashraf sat quietly in the back-seat, waiting patiently for whatever Anant had in mind.

'Let's give it a bit more time,' Anant suggested.

It was after another half an hour that Anant suddenly sat up in his seat. 'Now... go slowly... keep following that man,' he told Rego.

Rego eased the car into motion. He still had his sunglasses on. Although there were only a few vehicles at that time of the night, the narrow road appeared more congested than it actually was. The man Anant had pointed to was wearing a light-coloured, full-sleeved shirt and dark trousers. He was walking slowly, almost mechanically, away from the shelter. When the car was almost twenty feet behind him, Anant signaled Rego to stop the car. He got down and started following the man on foot. Anant had to slow down his pace to maintain an adequate distance between him and the man. Rego parked the car where Anant had gotten down.

The man took a right turn at the next junction, and continued walking. Anant followed him, and glanced behind. They would not be visible from the shelter now, if anyone was watching. He quickened his pace and caught up with the man. When he was a step behind him, he tapped him on the shoulder. The man jumped and turned behind, and was shocked to see Anant.

'Sir, you!'

'Keep walking with me. I want to have a chat,' Anant told the security guard from the shelter. The man obeyed without objection.

'So, this is the time your shift normally ends?' Anant asked.

'Yes, sir... around this time... I leave after the night-shift guard reports for duty.'

Anant nodded. 'I think you know something about Ryan's disappearance. Do you want to tell me?'

'Sir... I don't know anything... believe me,' the man replied, his face pale with fear.

'It's a little boy we are talking about. We were lucky to have found him alive, but anything could have happened. So, please tell me everything you know. It may seem unimportant to you, but tell me anyway.'

They had turned away from the main road, and the lane was almost deserted. Anant realized they were walking along the boundary of the playground, on the opposite side of the shelter.

'Sir, I am not sure... I don't want to get anyone in any trouble.... Nor do I want to get into any.'

'Nobody will get into trouble unless they have done something wrong,' Anant replied in a stern voice.

The security guard sighed. 'Sir, this is not the first child that has gone missing from Baby Steps.'

'What?' Anant could not believe his ears.

'Ryan is the third. By God's grace, you found him, but the other two...,' the guard's voice trailed off, as he shook his head sadly.

'And who do you think is behind all this?'

'Sir, I am not sure... so.....'

'Go ahead, tell me,' Anant said reassuringly.

'This Omkar... I suspect he has something to do with the missing kids.'

'Why do you say that?'

'I saw him with Ryan that evening... after all the other kids had returned.'

'What else?' he asked.

'Even with the other two children who disappeared... somehow, I remember seeing them alone with Omkar on many occasions. It may be nothing, but...'

'You have been a great help,' Anant patted the man on the shoulder. 'What about Mrs D'sa? What do you think of her?'

'She and Omkar are very close, sir... I don't know anything beyond that.'

***

'I think we may have got something,' Anant told Ashraf and Rego as he climbed back into the police car. He recounted his conversation with the security guard.

'But if that is the case, why did they file a police complaint when Ryan went missing?' Ashraf asked.

'I don't think they would have. It was only when our friend, the day security guard, resumed duty the next morning and insisted on filing a complaint, that it was filed.'

'And no complaint was filed for the other two kids?'

'Nope. Unfortunately, nobody missed them, and our man must have raised his voice this time.'

'And Omkar – where is he now?'

'With the police getting involved, he must have fled... he will lie low for some time, I think,' Anant deduced. He dialled Omkar's number again, but it was still unreachable.

'I will keep an eye out for him,' Rego offered.

'Yes, that will be useful,' Anant nodded.

'Should we question Mrs D'sa further?'

'I don't think we will get anything. We simply run the risk of alerting Omkar, if she is also involved.'

Anant thanked Rego for his help, and promised to stay in touch. The case may bring them to Goa again, after all. Anant retired to his room; they had an early morning flight the next day. He looked at his phone, and clicked open the picture he had taken at Mrs D'sa's office. Anant pinched the photo to enlarge Omkar's face, whose cold, piercing eyes stared back at him. Anant wondered if he had found a solid lead in the case.

22

Hong Lin walked by the lake in Beihai park and stopped when he heard squeals of laughter. He looked at the two children – a boy and a girl – in the pedal boat. The boy, who looked older but not more than ten, had leaned down over the side of the boat and was splashing water on the little girl. An older man, the father, he presumed, had stopped pedaling and was clicking pictures of them. Lin smiled; he had pleasant childhood memories of the Beihai park. And a couple of photographs as well. But that was two decades ago. He loved the park; it was his favourite place in the city. He walked there every week, always by the lakeside, watching Beijingers enjoy boating in the warm lake in summer, and skate on it when it froze over in winter. For the past two years though, the pleasure he used to derive from his walks in the park had been marred by the compulsion of the activity every Saturday evening.

It was a warm evening, and Lin wore a half-sleeved tee over his faded denims and sneakers. Thanks to his clean-shaven, boyish face, he looked much younger than his thirty-six years. Born to lower middle-class parents, Lin's only ambition in life was to become rich. And it was that ambition which had gotten him in this predicament. He sighed and shook his head, as he continued walking.

He passed under a bridge, and saw that the familiar bench was unoccupied. It usually was, owing to the distinct stench of urine that surrounded the area due to people relieving themselves under the bridge. As was his ritual, he sat down on the left edge of the wooden bench, his left hand placed casually on the arm-rest. He sat there for a few minutes, casually looking around him. When he was certain nobody was paying attention, with his right hand, he felt the plank underneath the seat. As on most days, he did not expect to find anything, except that day, his fingers felt a protruding object. He unglued the packet that was stuck to the underside of the bench. It was no bigger than a shampoo sachet, and looked like one, too. While seated, he slid it into his back pocket. He sat there for another ten minutes, after which, he walked back home. His heart was pounding so loud he was sure it could be heard by the other park-goers.

An hour later, Lin reached his modest apartment. Once inside, he double-checked the lock on the door, and opened the packet. It was a piece of paper, neatly folded to fit inside the small sachet. He wondered what the instructions would be this time. He swore under his breath as he read the note. *How did I get into this mess?* he cursed. He walked to the refrigerator, took a swig of cold water, and sighed. He sat down on the sofa and switched on the television, but his mind wandered off to that fateful day when it all started.

***

Two years ago, while on a business trip to Hong Kong as a part of a delegation, Lin had taken off to Macau one afternoon, having wrapped up with work early. No harm combining business with a little bit of pleasure, he thought. The evening had started well for Lin at the Venetian, Macau. In just a couple of hours, he was up by more than twenty thousand dollars at the Blackjack table. *This is my day,* he told himself. Lin grew more confident, and upped the stakes. He felt invincible, and incredibly lucky that day. And today, even after two years, Lin could remember exactly when he took the decision to double down.

He finished his drink, went to his room and opened the safe. He looked at the wad of notes. *Five hundred thousand dollars.* He promised himself that he would stop when he was up to a million. He never, even once that evening, thought that he could lose the money which was not even his to start with.

Lin exchanged the cash for chips and went to the same table; his seat was occupied by a fat Chinese woman. He decided to wait for his 'lucky' seat. After fifteen minutes, the game stopped momentarily as a new dealer took over, and the woman walked away with a resigned look on her face. Lin quickly took the seat, and smiled at the new dealer, a good-looking young woman with Asian features. Lin won the first three games in a row; and grew bolder. Over the next two hours, he lost more games than he won, and for the first time that evening, his earnings dipped to a negative. Lin decided to make up for the losses, and increased his bets. It was four in the morning, and Lin was the only player at the table, when he lost his last chip.

'Hard luck, sir,' said the dealer, now a burly Caucasian man, in an unsympathetic tone.

Sweat trickled down Lin's face into his eyes, stinging them, and announcing his fear. 'Having a bad evening?' a voice next to him said.

Lin looked up to see a middle-aged Indian man, who had just arrived, and was sitting next to him at the table. The portly man, formally dressed, looked inquiringly at Lin over his rimless spectacles. 'Let me offer you a drink, young man,' he said, and got up, beckoning Lin to join him at the bar. Lin remained seated, wiping his forehead with a handkerchief. 'Come on, I can help you,' the Indian said, gently nudging Lin on the shoulder.

Unsure, but without any other alternative, Lin joined the Indian, who led him to a quiet corner at the bar. Over the next hour, the Indian explained to Lin what he wanted. Lin kept looking down most of the time, shaking his head slightly from time to time.

'Okay,' Lin said softly at the end of their discussion.

'Great, here you are,' the Indian said, as he opened his leather briefcase and handed Lin a briefcase. 'It's enough to make up for your losses tonight.'

Lin sighed, and accepted the briefcase grudgingly.

'I will be in touch,' the Indian said, and got up to shake hands with Lin. Lin smiled slightly and turned to go.

'One last thing,' the Indian called out after him. Lin stopped and looked back. 'Just in case you change your mind, remember this,' the Indian said, and showed him his phone. There were pictures of the two of them. *Talking. Sitting together. The Indian handing over the briefcase to Lin.*

'I understand,' Lin said softly, like an animal backed into a corner.

'I am sure you do.'

When Lin was out of earshot, Robin Dutta dialled a number and said to the listener at the other end, 'It's done, sir. We have our asset.'

***

Lin woke up in the present; the television was on, and the remote was still in his hand. He played Robin Dutta's note in his mind again. The RAW officer had a follow-up question on the information Lin had passed on. *Who is the woman? Need details urgently.*

That will be difficult to find out, Lin thought. As the official spokesperson of the Chinese foreign ministry, he did have access to information. But in this case, he very much doubted if Chen Jintao, his boss, had an *actual file* on the woman. He would just have to keep his eyes and ears open. But the problem was, Robin wanted the information urgently. And that increased his risk of exposure. *And Chen Jintao was not known to be merciful towards traitors.* He knew the consequences of being exposed as a traitor very well.

23

With the general elections around the corner, planned to be held in September-October that year instead of the usual April-May, Ajit Raut was working round the clock. Along with Pawar, he was in-charge of the election campaign for Adhikari. All election forecasts projected a resounding victory for the IPP, much to the relief of the party top brass. There was some initial disbelief, and trepidation, when Doshi had announced his plans to retire from active politics, which was immediately after his return from Davos in January. Adhikari was, after all, a strong regional leader at best, with little experience in national politics. But under Doshi's oversight, Jha, Goswami and Mahajan had charted out a solid campaign strategy for Adhikari; and Raut and Pawar were heading its execution. Doshi himself was actively campaigning for Adhikari, and with every passing day, not only was Adhikari's popularity increasing among the masses, but his acceptance within the party was also getting stronger.

With Adhikari's victory now a foregone conclusion, Raut was getting ready to make the shift to New Delhi. According to him, it was the same ball-game, albeit with different players. He was in Delhi for a fund-raiser for the campaign; having arrived the same morning. He had proceeded directly to meet with Jha. It was only his second meeting with the home minister, after which, he realized that it would take him some more time to break the ice with the veteran politician. But he was prepared to wait; it would be worth it to have an ally as powerful as Jha.

The fund-raiser was a high-tea event at the Imperial, a heritage five-star hotel nestled in the heart of Delhi. Raut had booked a room at the same hotel to avoid unnecessary commuting within the capital. After finishing his morning meetings, Raut checked in at the hotel just before the event was scheduled to commence. He changed quickly and rushed down to the banquet hall. A few invitees were already there. He saw the familiar faces of Goswami and Mahajan, and walked towards them.

'Raut, how are you?' Mahajan asked, smiling genially.

'Very well, sir, thank you. Nice to meet you,' Raut replied.

He was in awe of the septuagenarian, and looked forward to learning the ropes of national politics from him. Mahajan patted him on the shoulder. Goswami, on the other hand, gave him a curt nod.

'Excuse me, I will join you in some time,' Goswami said, and walked towards an old man enjoying his coffee, who Raut recognized as a well-known pharma industrialist. He had sensed Goswami's unease, and at times, his cold attitude towards him. Of course, he acted courteous and warm in the presence of Doshi and Adhikari; but in spite of that, Raut could feel his unease.

'It's natural,' Mahajan told Raut, following his gaze, which was still focused on Goswami.

'I am sorry, sir. I didn't understand,' Raut said, turning towards Mahajan.

'His boss is retiring; and his future is uncertain. He sees you as a threat to his career.'

'I can understand his anxiety, but I do genuinely value his experience.'

'I know that. I think Adhikari has to talk to him to allay his fears. He can be a great asset to the new team.'

'I will convey the message, sir. Thank you,' Raut said. Mahajan's ongoing advice would be very useful for the new prime minister.

'Come, let's enjoy the event,' the old man smiled.

The evening went off better than expected. Raut hobnobbed with the who's who of the corporate world, many of whom he was meeting for the first time. He observed that no alcohol was served in the event; an old trick to keep the potential donors sober enough to sign fat cheques. The last of the invitees had left by 7 p.m., and Raut walked across to where Jha and Mahajan were standing. They stopped their conversation as soon as Raut joined them; he gathered they were discussing the likely donations coming their way – the collections of the evening.

'It went quite well, I think,' Devika Naidu joined the trio. She was accompanied by her husband, Rajan. Raut smiled and extended his arm to Rajan, who gave him a cursory handshake without making eye contact.

'Come, let's sit and talk,' Jha said, and led the group to a sitting area in one corner of the hall. Goswami, too, walked over.

'The *honourable* chief minister did not make it to the event?' Devika asked, her tone oozing with sarcasm.

'*We* all are here to work for him,' Jha laughed.

'Of course,' Devika retorted. Mahajan gave her a stern look, and changed the subject. 'Let's order some food.'

'I'll get myself a drink,' Rajan said and left for the bar, which was now open. Raut, sensing an opportunity to strike a conversation with Rajan, followed him.

'How are you, Rajan?' Raut asked, standing next to Rajan at the bar counter.

'Oh, it's the powerful Mr Raut! What do you have for me today, sir?' Rajan said.

'Come on, Rajan,' Raut forced a smile, trying to make light of the comment.

A year ago, as a part of his plans to open a chain of hotels in India, Rajan had proposed Mumbai for their first. He, along with his Russian partner, had met Adhikari to present the proposal. Raut and Pawar were also present in the meeting as the ministers for Urban Development and Finance & Planning respectively. As always, Adhikari had relied on his two lieutenants for inputs before he took the final decision.

As the proposed location for the hotel was in the heart of central Mumbai, Raut had insisted on three floors of exclusive public parking space. Under the Mumbai 2030 charter, he had made it a mandatory requirement for all new constructions; a price the city had to pay for rampant, unplanned development in the past decade. It was unacceptable for Rajan. *We cannot let any Tom, Dick or Harry enter our five-star property. And there are added costs and security concerns, he had argued.*

Pawar's condition was to employ local, state staff, to which Rajan had readily agreed. But due to Pawar's second requirement of providing commensurate employment benefits to all part-time and gig economy workers as well, Rajan's financial projections were going completely haywire. *Such benefits are not even offered in the most developed of countries,* he reasoned.

After much deliberation, Adhikari stuck to the two conditions put forth by Raut and Pawar. And the deal fell through. It also soured, to a large extent, the relations between Rajan and the Russian conglomerate, who lost faith in his abilities as a mover and shaker. The whole of the past year, Rajan was trying to mend the relationship, while scouting for a suitable location for their venture. Devika as the prime minister would have solved the matter for him, and opened up new doors at the same time.

'Your usual, sir,' the bartender placed a glass of Russian vodka with three cubes of ice and a dash of lime in front of Rajan.

'Life is a two-way street... never forget that, Raut,' Rajan said icily, picked up his glass and walked away. Raut gulped and stared after him.

'Anything for you, sir?' the bartender asked Raut.

'No, thank you. Just a glass of water please.'

Raut took the glass and walked back to where the group was seated. As the staff served snacks, the group chatted away. No new jibes were taken, but Raut continued to feel like an outsider. He could feel the indifference, bordering on hostility, simmering beneath the courtesy. *It's going to take a lot of time to sort this out,* he thought.

'I think I will retire to my room. I have an early morning flight back to Mumbai,' Raut said, and excused himself.

He was exhausted, and crashed on the sofa in his room. He was also famished; he had hardly eaten anything earlier. He quickly went through the in-room dining menu, dialled room-service and ordered in. He thanked the polite staff and hung up, hoping that the food would be delivered sooner than the thirty minutes he was promised. He was looking around for the television remote, when the bell to his room rang. He saw through the peep-hole; it was a room service staff. He opened the door.

'Sorry to disturb you, Mr Raut,' the bespectacled young lady said. She was dressed immaculately in staff uniform, her hair tied in a tight bun. The golden name badge on her dress read 'Tara'. She was carrying an ornate wooden tray in her hands. The tray was covered with a red silk cloth.

'I hope you are having a good stay with us, Mr Raut,' she said, walking into the room.

'Yes, very much. Thank you, Tara.'

'Your friends have sent these chocolates for you,' she explained, as she uncovered the tray to reveal three exquisite bars of dark chocolate.

'My *friends*?' he asked.

'From the banquet hall,' the lady said, giving Raut a dazzling smile.

'Ah, yes, of course. Thank you very much,' Raut said, pleasantly surprised.

'Is there anything else I can help you with, sir?'

'No, everything is perfect.'

'Have a good evening, sir,' the lady said, and left. Raut closed the door behind her, and smiled. *It is a nice gesture. I guess they are warming up,* he thought.

He looked at the chocolate bars. It was a brand that Raut did not recognize. He spent a few seconds choosing between the three flavours before deciding on the orange bar. He slid the bar out from the brightly printed sheath. The chocolate was wrapped in silver foil. It was when he broke one end of the chocolate bar that Ajit Raut died.

24

Upon hearing the news, Adhikari flew into Delhi on a chartered flight, along with Pawar and Dalvi. Anant, post his return from Goa, was following up on the kidnapping angle when news of Raut's killing reached him. Suspecting a terror attack, his cop instinct after years with the ATS led him to join Adhikari and team to Delhi. *Were the two cases linked? Were multiple cities the target of the same conspiracy?*

It was almost midnight by the time they had arrived at the Imperial, which was in chaos. The road leading to the hotel and its entrance were bustling with media activity. Reporters, who were covering the news 'live', clamoured around every vehicle that was allowed in the premises of the hotel. Media was not allowed to enter the hotel, however, and that eased the situation inside to a large extent.

The entire 11th floor of the Imperial, where Raut's room was, had been cordoned off, and all the guests on that level were offered alternate accommodation in the hotel. However, many panicked guests were in the lobby, wanting to check out as quickly as possible. The hotel staff and management were trying their best to assuage their fears and calm them down, but with little success. The cops finally prevailed and managed to clear the lobby. Jha, with his heavy security cover, was deep in discussion with the Delhi police commissioner when Adhikari walked in with his entourage.

Anant, after getting a quick update from the commissioner, went up to Raut's room, escorted by the hotel manager. The room, with its door closed, looked like any other room on the floor from the outside. It was when Anant stepped inside that he saw the extent of the wreckage. It was as if a huge bite had been taken out of the centre of the room. There were pieces of glass, wood and metal strewn on the floor, intermingled with human remains. It took Anant some time to gather his wits.

'How did you discover it?' Anant asked the manager, who was looking queasy.

'Mr Raut had placed an in-room dining order, but did not open the door when our staff went to deliver it. The staff alerted us when he smelled a burning odour.'

'And the fire alarms did not go off due to the smoke?'

'No, uh... they didn't... we're not sure why,' the manager shrugged, looking embarrassed.

A unit of the BDDS, the Bomb Detection and Disposal Squad, was in the process of scanning every inch of the room using the grid technique[1].

Anant, too, joined the team, having introduced himself to the unit-in-charge. After an hour of work, evidence was still being collected and labelled. Anant pointed to a thin metallic plate, around six inches in length, and asked, 'What is this?'

'Most likely the IED,' the unit-in-charge said, pointing to the charred etchings and miniature devices attached to the plate. 'We are analysing it... give us a couple of hours.'

'How did it get here?' Anant asked, thinking out loud. 'Let's check the CCTV footage,' he told the hotel staff and left the room.

***

'Do you see how distraught he is?' Jha pointed to Adhikari. He had pulled Goswami to a corner.

---

[1] The 'grid' is a much-used crime scene investigation technique wherein the scene of the crime is divided into much smaller squares, like a chessboard. The investigators then look for evidence in each square, methodically moving from square to square horizontally and then vertically. Each square is assigned a grid number, and a map is constructed at the end of the search, referencing evidence to the grid number where it is found.

'Yes, he is quite shaken. His reliance on his two allies has always been high,' Goswami concurred.

'*High* is an understatement. I think without Raut, he will have a serious issue being functional. And with higher stakes, impossible.'

'He still has Pawar... and maybe he will find someone to replace Raut.'

'Don't be under any illusion that you are that person... and who knows how much longer Pawar will last,' Jha chuckled.

'I... I don't know what you mean,' Goswami said.

'Forget what I said. Just do this one thing for me,' Jha gestured Goswami closer.

'What?' Goswami said, as he nodded and took a step forward.

'You have the prime minister's ear. You must tell him this event has weakened Adhikari, and the country deserves a strong prime minister. There is still time to announce another name.'

'You mean... yours?'

'You are a smart man, Goswami. I leave that to you.' Jha smiled.

***

'Start from the morning,' Anant told the young man, probably in his early twenties, who was a part of the IT security department at the hotel. He was in a small office at the lobby level, along with the hotel manager. They were looking at the camera footage of the passage on Raut's floor on a computer screen. 'That is Mr Raut's room,' the manager said, pointing to a door to the left of the screen.

The IT official played the recording in fast-forward mode; the timer on the top right of the screen advanced a few minutes every second.

Around noon, two housekeeping staff made the rounds of the floor, servicing the rooms. They entered Raut's room as well. Anant looked at the manager, who said, 'Our check-in time is 2 p.m. Our standard practice is to make up the room before the guest arrives.'

Anant nodded. 'And was the room occupied, the previous day?' he asked.

'No, sir. It was vacant.'

'There he is,' Anant said, as he saw Raut going to his room in the afternoon. He left the room soon after, dressed in a different attire. Anant stood there, his hands folded across his chest, as the timer quickly advanced towards evening. Nothing. It was around 8:30 p.m. when the frail form of Raut reappeared on the screen. His head was down; he looked tired. 'Go easy now, don't fast forward,' Anant told the operator. 'Something has to happen now.'

There was complete silence in the room. Anant leaned forward, his face only inches away from the screen. Less than seven minutes since Raut had gone to his room, a figure emerged from the bottom of the screen, and walked slowly ahead in the passage. It was a woman, dressed in the hotel uniform, with her back towards the camera. From the way her hands were positioned, Anant could make out she was carrying something. She reached Raut's room, and stood there for a moment. With a quick glance behind, she rang the bell to his room. A few seconds later, the door opened and she went inside. As she turned to enter the room, Anant saw that she was bespectacled, and carrying a tray, its contents covered. She left the room soon after, and turning towards the camera, almost ran out the way she had come. She was looking down all the time.

'That's it,' Anant said. 'Stop, rewind.' Anant went through the footage at least a dozen times, pausing and enlarging frames. 'Is she from the hotel?' he asked the manager.

The manager thought for a while before replying, 'I don't think so, sir... she does not look familiar.'

'And how did she leave the hotel? Let's check the cameras near the lifts,' Anant said to the operator.

'I don't think she went out that way. The lifts are on the other side. This way,' the manager said, indicating to the bottom of the screen, 'is the staircase.'

'Let's check the staircases then,' Anant told the operator.

'No cameras there,' the operator said.

'Damn... but where does the staircase lead? She must have used some exit.'

'At the ground level, you can either come out from the staircase into the lobby; or keep going to the basement into the service area, where there's the warehouse, lockers and changing room for the staff and the laundry,' the manager explained.

'Show me the staff exit. From the same time,' Anant told the operator.

'Here is... camera nine,' the operator said, tapping on a part of the screen.

'Zoom it,' Anant told him.

The staff exit was a narrow, dimly lit walkway next to the service entrance of the hotel. It opened up on the main street. A security cabin stood between the two. The camera was fixed at a distance, and at a height. For the next ten minutes of the footage, there was no movement on the camera, except the silhouettes of the two guards in the cabin. Beyond that, the traffic on the street appeared to be busy as usual. Just then, two figures walked in. Anant squinted his eyes and leaned forward to get a clearer picture, but he could make out nothing more, except that the two were males. The two walked straight in, without being stopped at security. Anant looked quizzically at the manager. 'Staff,' the manager said, 'we have a change of shift at this time.'

Over the next few minutes, the two were followed by around a dozen staff, who walked into the hotel. And an equal number of people left the hotel, either alone or in pairs. Anant had the video paused to have a closer look at every person leaving. But the images were very blurred and grainy when zoomed in. Even the manager was not able to identify every staff member.

'Is there a CCTV on the street, where we could have a better look?' he asked the manager.

'No, sir. There is one at the junction, but that is after you make the turn.'

Anant sighed and shook his head. Just then, his phone buzzed. It was the unit in-charge of the BDDS.

'We've got something,' he told Anant.

*****

'An IED, an improvised explosive device,' the BDDS unit-in-charge said, 'can take any form and can be activated in a number of different ways.' He added the explanation looking at the perplexed faces of Adhikari and Jha.

'And this is the one?' Anant asked, pointing to the metal plate in the unit-in-charge's hand. It was the same one he had seen earlier.

'Yes, let me try and explain what happened... or at least, what I *think* happened. All IEDs typically require four components – the power source, an initiator, the explosive and a switch. In this case, all of these are here,' he said, moving his finger along the scorched surface of the plates. The trio looked carefully at the crisscross of burnt wires and a few dangling pieces of metal they could not recognize.

'But what is it?' Anant asked.

The unit-in-charge brought two other similar sized items, which were wrapped in a transparent plastic bag. The two new pieces were a colourful mix, predominantly black and brown, with some portions of the silver metal plate visible. It was evident that underneath the outer layer, the two were the same as the IED. 'And this,' he said, 'is the fifth component – the container... which, in this case, was a chocolate bar.'

'A chocolate bar?' Adhikari asked, surprised.

'Yes, it was a command-initiated IED, that is typically detonated when there is a human interaction with the triggering mechanism. In this case, the canvas trigger was pulled when the chocolate bar was broken, sending an impulse to the receiver, and the detonation was triggered... the semtex was ignited and the explosion took place,' the unit-in-charge concluded.

'More like a chocolate *bomb!*' Anant said.

'Who the hell are we dealing with here?' Adhikari thought out aloud.

25

It was almost 7 a.m. when the thin man reached Rajawadi hospital in Ghatkopar, a north-eastern suburb in Mumbai. The land on which the municipal hospital stood belonged to the royals of Baroda until 1950, when the BMC acquired the land and the hospital was constructed.

With a dark brown shawl wrapped over his shoulders and head, covering most of his face, the man, holding his right knee with one hand, limped to the entrance of the old structure of the municipal hospital. A discerning eye would have spotted that his wobbling walk was not only exaggerated, but also inconsistent. But the man passed the lobby of the hospital without attracting the attention of the sparse crowd. He made his enquiry at a shabby glass counter, behind which was a small pharmacy.

'206, second floor; but visiting hours start 9 a.m. onwards,' the indifferent staff told the man without looking at him too closely.

The thin man walked unsteadily through the empty corridor and sat down on a wooden chair opposite a staircase, and began his wait.

***

Anant was exhausted from his back-to-back trips to Goa and Delhi. He had not slept a wink in the last two nights. Raut's killing had shaken him to his core. Now that he knew for certain Raut was killed in a sophisticated terror attack, and upon seeing the CCTV footage, he wondered whether the two female suspects related to the two investigations might be one and the same. It all pointed to a much larger conspiracy, he was sure of that.

Anant had never seen Adhikari so distraught. The chief minister had shrunk in size overnight, after the passing of his trusted lieutenant. And the *way* he was killed. Adhikari had barely said a word to anyone since boarding the flight back to Mumbai. He hadn't even talked to Raut's wife, which Anant found strange, but he later got to know that he had planned to visit her personally to offer his condolences. After they landed in Mumbai, Adhikari decided to go home first. Anant figured he wanted to confide in his wife Manjiri about the death of one of his closest aides. He knew the two families were very close and his wife may want to accompany him as well to the deceased minister's family.

After exchanging a quick word with Adhikari, as he headed home from the airport, Anant decided to take a much-needed short rest; he could barely keep his eyes open. He hailed a taxi and fell asleep as soon as he sat inside. He was jerked awake within a few minutes as the taxi stopped at the toll exit. He realized he could not go home yet.

'Let's first go to Rajawadi hospital,' he told the cabbie.

***

It was almost 9 a.m. when Anant reached the hospital. After the Goa trip, he was keen to personally check on Ryan to see how he was doing. Anant loved children; his heart went out to the little boy, who he thought had escaped miraculously from the clutches of a miserable life, maybe even death. He had still not gotten over the loss of his unborn child. He knew Nandini hadn't, too. And now she was fighting every minute for her life as well.

'Wait here, I'll be back in ten minutes,' he told the cabbie. Anant stretched as he got out of the cab. He started to walk towards the hospital entrance, when he spotted a tea stall. *I could do with some chai,* he thought. The young boy at the stall handed him a transparent glass of the steaming, milky concoction. Anant took a sip and let out a contented sigh as he felt the warmth of the chai flowing through him. He instantly felt more awake.

***

At the stroke on nine, Omkar adjusted the shawl that covered his head, and got up. The ward boy opened the iron shutter at the staircase entry, and promptly walked away. Omkar rushed up the staircase, limping intermittently. *Ryan had to be taken care of.*

On the second level, the staircase opened in two directions. Omkar looked around the deserted corridor and turned right when he spotted a solitary policeman outside the room at the far end. Seated on a plastic chair, the cop looked up when he heard the shuffling sound of feet approaching him.

***

Anant reached the second floor, saw the signages, and turned towards room 206. From afar, outside the room, he saw the policeman on duty, slouched over his chair in a casual, lazy position. Anant shook his head; fewer sights annoyed him more than a policeman asleep on duty.

Irritated, he quickened his step. The figure slumped lifelessly to its left when Anant tapped him on the shoulders. That's when Anant saw the slit throat. The front of the cop's shirt was soaked in blood, which was still trickling out of the gash on his throat. The man was dead – Anant did not have to double-check.

Instinctively, he reached for his gun, but realized he had not carried one to Delhi. He cursed under his breath. His first thought was to call for backup, but he did not have time to waste. He prayed his fists would be enough against whatever armed menace was behind the door. Without making a sound, he opened the door to room number 206.

***

Once inside, Anant saw a faint outline of a figure through the opaque, plastic curtains that were fully drawn over the hospital bed. Through a tear in the curtains, he saw a man leaning over the little boy; he was about to bring down a pillow held tightly in his two hands over the boy's head to choke the life out of the tiny, helpless figure. Anant roared and drew open the heavy, stained curtains. The man turned around, clearly startled. One look at those piercing eyes and Anant knew who he was. *Omkar.*

Anant's fists were clenched; his entire body was shaking with barely suppressed rage. It was as if his trained physique had been switched on for action. Eyes on the man facing him, Anant moved forward, his heart hammering in his chest. To his surprise, the thin man did not step back; instead, the determined look in his eyes confirmed that he was ready for combat. Anant took a fleeting glance at the child – he was asleep, possibly sedated, but alive. A flash of relief passed over him when he threw the first punch. It slammed against Omkar's face, who staggered backwards under the impact.

Anant landed another one before Omkar could recover. Omkar crouched in pain, and sunk forward to Anant's stomach. Anant brought his right knee up, which caught his adversary on the chin. Omkar fell flat on his back, tearing down the curtains from the flimsy steel frame, which rattled and shook, but somehow, held its ground. As Anant moved towards Omkar, the thin man quickly shuffled up on his feet and faced him. Blood had pooled in his mouth; and he was cursing and fidgeting, moving back and forth. But he did not appear scared.

Omkar reached into his pocket and took out a switchblade and pressed the button on its side to reveal the glistening blade, still red with the policeman's blood. He advanced towards Anant, who took pause and retreated a step. The two men circled around the small room, bare except for the curtains, the bed and the medical equipment next to it. Anant drew Omkar away from the child, and stopped moving once he had taken position between Omkar and the bed.

Almost on cue, the two men dived at each other, each determined to take the other down. Omkar swung his blade-yielding hand furiously, hoping to catch Anant in one of the wild movements. Anant's mind was solely focused on avoiding the killer hand. Seeing Anant focused on his right hand, Omkar struck him with his left. Anant was unable to dodge the blow, and for a brief instant, his eyes widened, amazed at the power of the punch. Before Anant could recover his wits, Omkar managed to tilt his head back and slammed it into Anant's. Stars burst in Anant's vision as he was blinded by the hit. He shook it off and swung his arms sloppily to keep Omkar at bay.

'Take that,' shrieked Omkar and tried to plunge the knife into Anant's chest. At the last moment, Anant swerved, and brought his left arm forward, shielding his heart against the fatal blade. He grimaced in pain as the knife slashed his left shoulder. He could feel the warm liquid spurting out of his body, making its way down his back and forearm.

Omkar smirked at Anant infuriatingly; Anant growled and threw himself at him. Both men came crashing down to the floor. Blood buzzed in Anant's veins, but anger and determination had taken over his reflexes. He held Omkar's right hand under his left knee and placed his body weight squarely on his torso. Omkar gasped for breath, and his grip on the blade loosened momentarily. Anant shoved the blade away with his now bloodied left hand, the motion causing him to clench his jaw in pain. Anant grasped Omkar's head in both his hands and brought his knee down on his nose. He heard a blunt crack, as blood leaked from both of Omkar's nostrils with his nose twisted to the left. Omkar coughed, and blood sputtered out from his mouth.

Anant fell sideward and lay down on his back, holding his left arm, his heart thudding loudly. His entire body was throbbing as his life blood continued to leak out of his left shoulder. He felt the switchblade next to him, and he gripped it in his right hand.

He turned to look at Omkar, whose chest rose and sank with each shallow breath he drew in. Leaning on his right hand, Anant grunted as he pulled himself up. He stood bending forward, resting his hands on his thighs; his knuckles were bleeding as well. He could hardly feel his left arm now. He lifted his head and saw that the little boy was still unconscious. *Good for him*, Anant thought.

Anant was still slouched when he heard the sound behind him. He turned around to see Omkar scrambling away towards the other end of the room. Taken aback by this unexpected turn of events for a moment, Anant started to run after Omkar but slipped on the pool of blood that had accumulated on the floor. That moment's delay was enough for Omkar to gather momentum; he dashed through the glass window and disappeared from view. Anant ignored the shards on the floor, and looked out of the shattered window. Omkar was lying in a pool of blood on the concrete floor of the hospital compound. He was not moving.

Anant turned and ran out of the room, down the stairs. A few people, including two security guards, had gathered around the spot where Omkar lay. Anant jostled through them and froze when he saw Omkar's lifeless body. Anant wondered why Omkar killed himself; was it to protect someone or was he so scared of someone that he chose to take his own life? The dead man's eyes sliced through the crowd and found Anant, staring at him coldly.

26

Bandhu and Tamas were awake, watching the news of Raut's death on the television, when M entered the apartment. She had taken a midnight flight out of Delhi, arriving in Mumbai in the early hours of the day after killing Raut. Tamas smiled and gave her a thumbs up; she gave him a curt nod in return and went into her room, locking it behind her. She took out her new handphone, the one that Tamas had given her, and contemplated whether to make the call now or later. She opened her call history; there were calls only with one number. She almost dialled the number, but decided to take a much-needed hot shower first.

Her toes flinched when she stepped into the tiled shower area. As the hot water soaked into her skin, she closed her eyes, and a hundred images crossed her mind. She pushed them aside and focused on the smiling face of Andrey. It had been years since she had seen him, or even spoken with him.

M grabbed a towel from the rack. Steam had filled the room; she dried herself and wiped the mirror. A stranger stared back at her. She was always taken aback when she saw the *real* her. She was still young, and good-looking, not strikingly beautiful though. And she was thankful for that. In her trade, it helped to be unremarkable.

After slipping into a comfortable cotton tee and pajamas, she felt as good as new. The two men were probably asleep; the lights were off and there was no sound. She made herself a sandwich, and retreated into her room again. She was about to bite into the sandwich when her phone buzzed. She instinctively looked at her burner, but the instrument was dark and silent. She had not activated the other phones. It couldn't be. But the buzzing did not stop. She looked inside her purse. *Her* phone was ringing. She answered it, her hand shivering. It couldn't be...*him.*

It was.

'I was waiting to see when you would use it... my favourite... you remembered,' Andrey said. *The Chocolate Bomb.*

It took M a few moments before she could muster the courage to speak. 'I haven't forgotten anything,' she managed finally.

'I have been following your exploits; you have done me proud.'

'I... How are you?' M said, relieved that Andrey was keeping track of her work. *Of her.*

'M... be careful,' Andrey said, and disconnected.

'Hello... hello,' M said, checking out the phone screen to see if the call was still on. But Andrey was gone. But she felt good that he had called. *He still remembers me.* But it was uncharacteristic of him to warn her. *Had the past few years blunted his killer instincts? Or did he know something that she didn't?*

She pushed the plate with the uneaten sandwich away and lay down on her bed, thinking about Andrey. M tossed and turned, unable to sleep. After sometime, she gave up. She looked at the time. It was 4:30 a.m. She dialled the number.

'That was good work,' said the Serpent, picking up the call at the second ring.

'I wanted to know why the change in plans?' M asked.

'Oh, there is no change in the overall plan... just a slight detour. Let's see if it takes us to the destination faster,' chuckled the Serpent.

M didn't understand what that meant, but knew better than to ask any more questions. It didn't matter to her as long as she was getting compensated for her 'additional efforts.' She was just curious.

'So, are you ready for the next move?' asked the Serpent.

'I'm all ears.' M smiled.

M could feel her heart beating faster, as she listened to the Serpent's instructions. Her eyes shone with excitement when he had finished. She pushed open the door to Tamas's room and switched on the lights.

'What the fuck!' Tamas shouted and pulled the duvet up to cover his face.

'Get up, there is work to do. And we don't have time,' M said calmly.

27

Anant was seated on a low bed in a medical room on the ground floor of Rajawadi hospital. The room was dimly lit, and green cloth curtains were half-drawn around the bed. A young doctor, probably an intern or resident, was hustling around him. She finally gathered her medical kit and placed it on the bed next to Anant. She smiled at him, and gently helped him remove his blood-soaked shirt. A deep wound had sliced the flesh of his left shoulder. Anant glanced at the mirror to the side to see a bluish-purple bruise forming around it. He knew the scar would remain with him until the day he died. As the doctor used an antiseptic tissue to clean the wound, the bleeding that had slowed down to a trickle, oozed out freely. Anant sucked in a sharp breath as the pain vibrated through his entire body. The doctor cleaned the wound thoroughly and wrapped a bandage around it.

'All done. The dressing will have to be changed tomorrow,' she told Anant. 'Thank you,' Anant smiled, and put on his shirt. He climbed down from the bed, and stood up unsteadily on his feet. Slowly, he made his way to the washroom. He was startled to see his tired features staring back at him through puffy eyes. He splashed water on his face with his good hand, and instantly felt better. In spite of his condition, he felt lucky not to have died that day.

He walked slowly to the pharmacy and bought the painkillers that he had been prescribed. He popped in two pills and gulped down an entire bottle of water. As he exited the hospital, the cops outside the casualty ward saluted him. Anant had called them after Omkar, or rather, his body, was taken in. In his entire career, Anant had not witnessed a shorter journey from the scene of the accident to the emergency ward of a hospital.

Once the local cops had arrived, Anant had retrieved Omkar's phone. While the phone was password protected and he would need help from the cyber-cell to unlock it, he saw a notification pop up on the locked screen. It was a message from Mrs D'sa. *'Have you taken care of the boy?'*

Anant felt relieved that Omkar's death was not another dead end.

***

Mrs D'sa felt very nervous; there had been no communication from Omkar since they had spoken the day the police had come to the shelter. He should have completed the job by now. She had expressed her reservations about the new, unknown client. Of course, the money offered was substantially more than usual, but came with its share of risk, which she was averse to. Unlike other traffickers, she did not have to use violence, manipulation, or false promises of well-paying jobs or romantic relationships to lure her unsuspecting victims. *They were right there with her. Trusting her; and the shelter.* At times, she had to answer questions from the children about their missing friends. And with little difficulty, she always convinced the unwary. *He has a new family now. She has moved to her new home. He will visit us very soon.* Her made-up stories would always raise hope in the eyes of the children who longed for the warmth of a family.

Mrs D'sa dialled Omkar's number one more time. It was switched off; she frowned. She wished she had not given in to Omkar's persistence. She wondered who the woman was that Omkar had delivered Ryan to. And why had she *left* the boy on the train?

The smiling face of Ryan appeared before her eyes momentarily, but she was quick to dismiss the image. She had crossed that bridge a long time ago. It had to be done. It was the third time in the last thirteen years that she had to resort to this course of action. *Or was it the fourth?* She had stopped keeping count.

She wiped her thick glasses with her handkerchief, and put them on. There was a moment of surprise, and then fear, when she saw the cop with sunglasses come into focus.

28

Bandhu felt good, although he was sweating like a horse in the intense humid weather. Mumbai was waiting for its first monsoon shower of the season. He could have easily outrun the group, but he eased his pace and continued running with them. It was the last of the fifteen kilometres they had to cover that Sunday morning, the second of June. Just a few months ago, he would have balked at the idea of running such a distance, in fact, running itself. But now he relished it. Breathing steady, heart strong, he felt as if he was born to run. He surely counted on it to save his life in less than a month from now.

A fellow-runner followed the group's pace without complaint, but was stumbling behind, his parched, rasping throat was evidence of his exhaustion. His springing steps, long disappeared, now pounded the tarmac gracelessly. Bandhu swiftly took out his water bottle from the belt around his waist and offered him a sip, which the man gratefully accepted. With the last two hundred metres remaining, Bandhu broke off from the group and sprinted to the finishing point – Chhatrapati Shivaji Maharaj Park, popularly known as Shivaji Park to Mumbaikars. The largest open ground in the city, it was flanked on all sides by a *katta*, a continuous low kerb edge, that served as a makeshift seat. The walking track around the park was packed with joggers and walkers, young and old. On Sunday mornings, the park was especially crowded.

Bandhu sat down on the katta, next to the park's entrance on the western side. It was the designated stop for their running club, Striders. The club ran a rigorous physical fitness program for its members, especially coaching them for marathons. Due to its affiliations and tie-ups, members of Striders also got preferred entry to major running events, both domestic and international. Ranga was one of the first members of the club. In fact, he was a strong supporter of the club, and had even introduced it as a health and fitness partner to the employees of the Sethna group of companies. For the Mumbai marathon, Striders was the fitness partner and also one of the associates managing the event. Bandhu had joined the club recently and through it, had secured entry into the marathon that year.

The rest of the group arrived at the katta, panting and sweating, but with a smile on their faces at having completed the run. 'Hey Bandhu, thanks for the water.' Bandhu returned the fist-bump and nodded to his running mate. 'Got your confirmation and BIB[2] number?' the runner asked.

'Yes, got the confirmation email last night,' Bandhu smiled.

'That's great. Join us for coffee?' An extended conversation over road-side coffee was a regular post-run activity amongst running groups.

'Not today, man. Have to reach home early,' Bandhu said, glancing at his watch. It was almost eight; M and Tamas would have left by now. Today was a day of action, and he may be needed in case things did not go as per plan.

Just as he was leaving, their running coach walked up to him. 'That was a good run, Bandhu. Keep it up and you'll surely hit your target on race day,' he praised, patting Bandhu on the back.

'That's the goal, coach,' Bandhu smiled, amused at the trainer's choice of words.

[2] The marathon BIB was a sheet of paper with an e-tag attached to it. The tag was used to record the runners' timing over the course of the marathon. The number was also printed on the BIB in large fonts, along with the runner's name. Once a runner's application for a marathon was confirmed, he was sent a confirmation and his BIB number for the run. Closer to the event, typically the weekend before, the participants collected their BIBs from specified collection centres.

29

The St. Xavier's College, located in the Fort locality of South Mumbai, was celebrating the completion of 150 years as the country's educational pioneer. The 150 years' celebration had been in the works for over a year, and alumni from all over the world were invited to participate over a week-long festival that was to start that day – the second of June.

Posters and banners proudly announced the celebrations along the entire road that led to the institution. Being a Sunday, traffic was lighter than usual, but the following days promised to be a nightmare, with the number of expected VIPs estimated at more than a hundred, spread over the course of the upcoming week. Three police vans stood outside the campus, with two more patrolling the road. No vehicles were allowed to park in the lane, and even drivers waiting in their vehicles were asked to move their cars away.

Ashraf walked towards the entrance of the college, where a few students were huddled, debating animatedly. They were dressed smartly in business formals; he assumed they were a part of the historic event's organising committee. He smiled at them. He hoped Naima too would be a part of Xavier's when she grew up. *But there's still time enough for that,* he reminded himself. The security guard stationed at the entrance stood up in attention as Ashraf passed him and went inside. As he crossed the lobby, he saw a group of cleaners, dressed in their standard uniforms, mopping the floor. A lanyard, that contained their identity card, hung around their necks. One of the cleaners, an old lady, her shirt two sizes too big for her hunched figure, side-stepped and turned in fluid motions with a mop in hand. She stopped abruptly as Ashraf approached closer. Looking down, she resumed her work once he had passed her by.

Ashraf stood in the open-air atrium, and looked around him. At one end of the atrium, a stage was set up. Both sides of the stage and the backdrop were decorated with props announcing 150 years' completion of the institution, making the stage appear larger than it was. The sound equipment was being tested; the lighting was set up at the periphery of the open area for the evening programs. The crew of the event management company looked worried and were busy giving finishing touches to the set-up. In front of the stage, seating was arranged on either side of a wide aisle. Ashraf estimated it to accommodate an audience of at least four hundred. Entry was restricted strictly to invitees, and students with identity cards. Students were also advised to occupy the seats at the back, and make way for other invitees if and when the situation demanded. Ashraf gestured to a cop, who was in discussion with the security-in-charge.

'Yes, sir,' the cop said as the duo walked up to Ashraf, who led them back towards the entrance of the college.

'I want the security check further tightened. Shut down the second entrance,' Ashraf said, pointing to the college gate to the left, 'and set up a dual check for the invite – one at the entrance and one here – before the lobby.'

The security officer looked at his watch. 'It's still one more hour to go, hurry up,' the cop told him. The officer took out his walkie-talkie and barked out some orders, as he hurried towards the left gate.

'Let's have two of our men as well at each of the entrances,' Ashraf told the cop.

'Sure, sir.'

'Okay, let's get to work,' Ashraf said. Hands on waist, Ashraf pursed his lips and looked around. Ever since Raut's killing, the ATS had been put on high alert, especially since the Thane shootout investigation was still ongoing. They knew they were racing against time, but had precious little to go after. Mrs D'sa's arrest in Goa had not yielded any further leads, and the pressure to solve the pending case was mounting by the day. This was one of the most high-profile events planned in the city, and the police were determined to leave no stone unturned to ensure it went off smoothly.

Although the college had cancelled all lectures for the week, the majority of the student body had turned up to participate in the festival. The inauguration was scheduled at eleven, and with an hour to go, small groups of youngsters started to gather in the atrium. Many of them still stood chatting in the corridors, or scattered around the campus. As some of the chattering bodies made their way down to the atrium, nobody paid attention to an old cleaning lady on her way up the staircase of the main building.

30

Placing his sweaty palms on the parapet of the terrace, sub-inspector Jagtap surveyed the scene below. He had been assigned the task to keep an eye on the proceedings from the top of the main building of the college. Four levels below, the atrium was quickly filling up with people. Most of the middle and back row seats were now occupied; the front seats were dotted colourfully with invitees in groups of threes and fours. A photographer had set up his tripod right in the centre of the aisle, between the first and the second rows. Six young crew members, each with a cordless microphone in hand, were lined up along the length of the court, ready to hand over the mic to anyone with a question once the session began.

Of the eight chairs on stage, the two at the centre were still vacant. A few minutes later, from directly below him, Jagtap saw a man in a black cassock emerge, and walk slowly across the atrium. Jagtap's gaze followed him, slowly moving to his right, as the dean of the college climbed the four steps onto the stage. The dean shook hands with the three men and three women on the dais and sat down on one of the empty seats at the centre. The group was now waiting for the chief guest to arrive.

Jagtap's khaki shirt, bulging around the waist, was damp and clung to his back. He stretched and walked over to the opposite side of the terrace, that overlooked the main road. He cursed under his breath as he dodged the lines of potted plants that took up most of the floor space. A crowd, hoping to catch a glimpse of a celebrity, had gathered on the street below. He wondered when the chief guest would arrive; it was his second day on duty in a row, without a break, and he wanted to go home as soon as this was over. He badly craved a nice, steaming cup of tea. *I could quickly grab one from the cafeteria,* he thought. He turned around to see an elderly lady stepping onto the terrace through the only door that led to it. For a moment, she looked as surprised when she saw him.

'Hey, who allowed you to come up here?' Jagtap asked, marching towards the woman.

'I just came to do my job, sir,' she said in a weak voice, clutching her backpack in front of her with both hands.

'There is no work today. You may leave,' Jagtap said, dismissing her with a wave of his right hand.

'Yes, sir,' the woman replied and dropped her bag.

Jagtap's eyes widened with fear as he stared at the revolver pointed at him. Before he could react, he was an inch off the ground. A neat, red hole in his heart oozed dark blood, and he crashed to the ground, his fall broken by an earthen flower pot.

M looked around her cautiously; she was sure there was nobody who could have seen the act. The silencer ensured nobody heard it, either. She was slightly uncomfortable leaving another dead body behind, but the policeman on the terrace was a complete surprise. She had no choice. But she did feel good when she used her revolver. She loved her work and her office for today was more than a century-old roof-top overlooking the exact spot where her target would soon arrive. She walked across to the other end of the terrace and retrieved a green cloth bag that was concealed amidst the thick shrubbery. For the last three days, when she came to 'work', she had been stashing away the various components of her M24 sniper weapon system.

She attached the sniper scope and the bipod to the barrel. The breeze was gentle; she would not have to make too many adjustments. Scanning the scene below through the telescopic lens, she saw the cop who had passed her in the lobby, and paused. Ashraf Siddiqui, the name badge read. 'One squeeze, and it will all be over for you, Mr Siddiqui,' she thought out loud. She smiled at how fickle life could be.

There was not enough noise from the atrium to suppress the sound of the firing, so she also attached a silencer. She had identified her exact position in a shaded area next to the water tank, to avoid exposure to direct sunlight; the glare of the sun could easily reflect off the scope, drawing attention to her position. As an additional measure, she had also covered the lens in a non-reflective material. That would be enough, she was certain.

She covered her ears with a hearing protection device, shaped like earmuffs. While a newer, upgraded version of the M24 was available, she preferred this one. It felt like an extension of herself. And she had never missed a target with it. She was ready. Now all she had to do was wait.

31

The dean beamed with pride at the turnout; he could see many of his now famous ex-students seated in the front rows. The atrium of his much-loved institution, where he had served for more than thirty years, was overflowing with alumni, students and his fellow colleagues. Top reporters from the media were also present to cover the inauguration of the celebration. The dean looked forward to personally thanking all the invitees later in the day. Two days back, when the police commissioner had spoken to him about the additional security arrangements, and the reasons for the same, he would be lying if he said he wasn't disturbed. But seeing how smoothly the event had progressed, his concerns were allayed, maybe even unfounded to begin with. The police presence and security checks – all seemed like standard protocol to the guests and the students.

It was five past eleven when the chief guest arrived at the St. Xavier's college. One of the event management crew members rushed up the stage and quietly informed the dean. The dean, along with the rest of his staff on the stage, stood up, as they saw the dignitary walk down the aisle. Two security guards walked a few steps behind the chief guest, as he laughed and shook hands with friends and batchmates. He warmly greeted the dean, who embraced his former pupil.

'Sorry, I am five minutes late. Am I allowed in?' he joked and asked the dean, who was infamous across generations for not allowing late arrivals entry to the college.

'Just this one time,' the dean laughed. 'I am so proud of you, my son.'

As the dean gave the inaugural address in his deep baritone, the crowd listened in rapt attention. A cacophony of applause and cheering, and palpable excitement buzzed through the charged air. There was a spontaneous outpouring of emotion at the accomplishments of their beloved institution and its alumni.

M had taken aim, and had the old man in the crosshairs. Her target was only partially in view, seated just behind the dean. She remained motionless in her position and waited for the dean to step aside. She didn't know how much time had passed, but realized the dean had concluded his address when he gestured with his right hand towards the chief guest, who got up and walked to the lectern.

Gautam Pawar now stood at the centre of the stage.

M took enormous pride in getting a good, clean kill. She had a reputation to maintain and that reputation guaranteed her exorbitant fee. She lay still; at her calmest, right before a kill. She had locked her target in the crosshairs. As Gautam Pawar flashed the crowd with a broad smile, M gently squeezed the trigger.

***

Pawar clutched the sides of the lectern for a split second before he was propelled backwards. As he fell flat on his back, the dean, along with the minister's security staff rushed to him. The bullet wound, dead centre to his heart, was not easy to see at first, until blood started oozing out of the neat hole in his vest.

In the moments that followed, there was a mixed reaction amongst the confused audience. A few hurried towards the stage out of curiosity or in an attempt to help. Some of them just stood there gaping, not knowing what had happened and unable to decide what to do next. But it was not long before fear struck the hearts of those in attendance, and the terrified crowd scurried towards the exit. Some were in the grip of silent panic, while some others were shrieking.

Ashraf, his brain screaming, dashed towards the stage, running as fast as his legs could manage. He could feel a tightening, uncomfortable sensation in the pit of his stomach. *No, no, no, this cannot be happening,* he wanted to shout out. One look at the collapsed man, and Ashraf knew the ambulance would be of no use.

***

M did not wait to see the aftermath of the assassination. She knew the bullet had done its job. She dismantled her sniper gear and shoved it in the backpack. She sprinted down the staircase. It had been less than thirty seconds since she had fired the shot. There was nobody on the third level. On the second level, she saw a few students gathered at the windows in a classroom, overlooking the atrium, peeping below. Some of them had their mobile phones out, and were clicking pictures and filming videos. None of them paid any attention to her. She could hear the uproar on the levels below as she descended down the second level. She slowed down, hunched forward, and holding the wooden railings of the stairway, made her way into the multitude. Now she was nothing more than a part of a moving mass, and in the given circumstances, one who was behaving quite predictably.

The crowd flowed forward, shoving and jostling, making its way into the wide corridor leading to the exit. The corridor was inundated with escaping people from two more connecting lobbies in addition to the staircase. M, clutching her backpack in front of her, was pushed forward by the horde that seemed to be locked in thought as much as their feet. As the crowd cleared the grilled exit, they ran helter-skelter down the college drive-way, towards the street. M resisted the temptation to run and kept up with her character, hurrying out as fast as an old woman could.

Ashraf ran past her, speaking on his mobile phone. A few other men in uniform followed him, shouting and shunting people aside. There were gasps of horror as people saw the blood-soaked body of Gautam Pawar being brought out on a stretcher. The crowd parted as an ambulance, its sirens blaring, made its way to the scene. All hell had broken loose. As students and guests rushed out of the college premises, a smaller crowd of policemen and first responders struggled to rush into the institution.

A short distance away from the college, an old lady hopped into the front passenger of a waiting car.

32

'How could this happen?' Sarathi was pacing nervously in his office. 'And whoever did this, how did he get away?'

'She,' Anant asserted softly, sucking in a deep breath. Inspite of Nandini's protests and against the doctor's advice, he had flown back to Goa the same day Omkar had died. Rego had arrested Mrs D'sa, and she was the only breakthrough they had in the case so far. Anant wanted to personally lead the interrogation. After three days of grilling, the old lady had broken down under pressure; but she was not of much help. Anant was convinced Mrs D'sa had no clue about the identity of the woman who had met Omkar. But her involvement in the child trafficking racket was proven without any doubt. She was put away for good.

The embarrassed state government had sprung into action, expressing deep anguish over the issue. The good news was, a local NGO, Child Welfare Society of Goa, had been appointed by the state government to take over the daily operations of the shelter. A reasonable monetary grant had also been promised to the NGO, a part of it released as well, to manage the initial expense.

Anant requested Rego to keep an eye on the transition, and he returned to Mumbai as soon as Ashraf had called him, and had headed directly to the ATS headquarters.

'There were more than five hundred people present... it was impossible to control the panicked crowd... within a few minutes, a majority of them had dispersed,' Anant said. He had taken a full account of the situation from Ashraf. 'The bullet was fired from the terrace of the main building.'

'How do we know that?' Sarathi asked.

'The body of SI Jagtap was found on the terrace when we scanned the premises.'

'Any other clue?'

'Not yet... the teams are still working on it... except...'

'Except?'

'Both Raut and Pawar were close confidants of Adhikari. He was heavily dependent on them – both politically and I believe, personally as well. Adhikari becoming our next prime minister is almost certain, and Raut and Pawar would have played an important role in national politics, supporting Adhikari,' Anant explained.

'Wait a minute... are you saying there is a political hand in these killings?'

'I wouldn't rule it out, sir.'

Sarathi sat down at his desk, and fidgeted with his pen. 'But how does this fit in with the China story? If this is – somehow – political, there is no connection between these two killings and the tip-off from RAW,' he said, not very convinced with Anant's theory.

'In fact, now I am more confident than ever they are interlinked. The RAW tip-off, given to them by their asset in China, was about a terrorist attack from someone in the train from Goa. Now we know that 'someone' is a lady. Raut was delivered the 'chocolate bomb' by a lady, who I believe was the same as the one in the train. That's the clear linkage. And now Pawar is killed – maybe by the same lady – which, I accept, is unknown as of now. Also, just look at the way Raut and Pawar were killed. Both the killings have been elaborately planned and executed by a professional, with access to resources. And if my theory is correct, a likely Chinese connection.'

'China?'

'Partly, yes,' Anant said.

'Why *partly*?'

'According to me, China on its own could not have gone through *this* sequence, nor would it have all the information required to carry it out... Raut's Delhi visit, while scheduled in advance, was known only to a few people... his fondness for chocolates was known to even fewer.... Pawar gave his confirmation to inaugurate the Xavier's event only last week. Someone with access to these details is feeding it to our lady friend.'

Anant continued, 'In their individual capacity, why would Raut and Pawar be targeted by anyone? One of them, maybe yes... but for both of them to get killed in quick succession, it leads me to believe the real target is somebody else. And that somebody is *Sanjay Adhikari*. Someone wants our future prime minister to die.'

33

Sanjay Adhikari was in his study, relaxing with a book when he heard the sound... A mournful wail. He stopped reading, and waited. Again, the faint sorrowful cry. He kept the book aside, and walked out of the study. The cries were louder now. They seemed to be coming from the lower floor of his duplex. He walked slowly along the carpeted floor of the corridor, and peeped over the railings.

In the large living area below, he saw a sea of people, all dressed in white. He hurried down the wooden staircase, and jostling through the crowd. He moved forward, searching for the source of the weeping sound. He kept on until he met with a sickening surprise. *It was Manjiri.* Clad in a white sari, she was crying inconsolably. Aashi was next to her. The mother and daughter were hugging each other, seated on the cold marble floor. A corpse, its face covered, was lying on the floor. Around it was a battery of guards; Dalvi was also standing with them. The throng of people looked down sadly at the shrouded corpse.

Adhikari walked up to Dalvi and asked him, 'Who died?' Dalvi dabbed his eyes with a handkerchief and replied, 'The prime minister.'

Adhikari gave him an incredulous look and knelt down next to the dead body. He reached for the thin, white cover and lifted it to get a look at the face of the person who had died in his house.

He screamed as he saw his own lifeless face staring back at him.

***

'Are you okay, Sanjay?' Manjiri asked, woken up by her

husband's scream.

'Yes... yes... just a bad dream,' Sanjay replied, wiping the cold sweat off his forehead. He could still feel the haunting presence of the crowd gathered at his own funeral.

'I cannot believe it... first Raut... and now Pawar,' he said, shaking his head. He sat crouched on his bed, breathing heavily. His mind wandered off to all the instances where he – *they* – had made enemies. And enemies they had made; there was no doubt about that. *But who could go to such extremes?*

Someone in the opposition? Unlikely.

A business partner who did not get a large contract? Possible. There was significant money to be made in large projects. Enough to kill for, too, if one did not get the business. He counted on his fingertips the projects that could qualify in this list. *The coastal road. The sea-link. The trans-harbour link. All marquee multibillion projects.* He shook his head. All applicants – awardee as well as the rejections – were reputed corporates from India and overseas. *Possible, but again unlikely.*

Wait a minute. What about the hotel project proposal by Rajan Naidu they had rejected? He knew that Rajan was in bed with some very nasty Russian partners. And Adhikari knew they were still struggling to get started in India. *Could it be the Russians? Or Rajan? Yes, that was quite likely.*

Just then, Manjiri turned on the lights, and put her arms around his shoulders.

'I feel so angry... my two closest aides and friends...' Sanjay exclaimed, throwing the duvet aside as he got up from the bed.

'Don't worry, everything will work out fine for us,' Manjiri reassured, her own voice not sounding very confident.

Sanjay nodded, and gave her a half-smile, loving his wife's unstinting support. Just then, his phone rang. It was the prime minister. Both of them were early risers, and frequently caught up first thing in the day, but never before had they spoken at five-thirty in the morning.

'Sanjay, how are you doing?' Doshi asked, his voice concerned. 'I am sorry to hear about Pawar.'

'Yes, it's difficult to comprehend what's happening... and who could be behind this,' Sanjay said, a hitch in his voice. He decided to voice his suspicions about Rajan when he met the prime minister in person.

'I know it's a huge personal loss for you. But whatever the party can do for you, and whatever I can do, we will do. So, try not to worry.'

'Thank you, sir, that means a lot to me.'

'One more thing, Sanjay. We are in the last leg of the elections. The opposition is too weak and fragmented... there is no doubt that we will win the elections,' Doshi said. Sanjay sensed the prime minister had more to say. He waited for him to finish. Doshi continued, his voice sterner, 'So, my advice is – keep your public appearances to a minimum now onwards. We cannot afford to take any risks. We should... we *need* to be more careful.'

'With due respect, sir, that will send a very wrong message to the party workers as well as the people at large. Nobody wants a leader who is scared. I have to keep up with my planned campaigns ... I cannot cancel even a single event off my itinerary.'

At the other end of the line, Doshi reflected on what his protégé had just said. That was exactly how he had thought – had known, rather – Sanjay would react. It was just his way of reaffirming his belief in his chosen successor. He was pleased to know that he had made the right decision. The double blow had not softened the prime minister-in-waiting.

***

After his early morning conversation with Sanjay, Doshi was comforted with his choice of successor, but he was also nervous. On one hand, the manner in which Raut and Pawar were killed suggested that a professional was at work. And the killer had the backing of someone with resources, and more importantly, information. He was increasingly convinced that an insider was involved. *A traitor? But who? Who could go to these extremes?*

On the other hand, he recognized that the ultimate target was Sanjay, and killing his two trusted lieutenants was only a way to get to him, to weaken him. How effective would Sanjay Adhikari be without his team? *That is, if Sanjay himself survived.* Doshi was agonizingly certain that an attempt would be made on Sanjay's life next. If something were to happen to Sanjay, who could be chosen to be the next prime minister of the country?

He opened his diary and looked at his schedule for the day. He had an early morning meeting with his core team. He decided to go for a quick walk before he got started with what promised to be yet another busy day. At seven-thirty, after a light breakfast, Doshi was already in his office. He reviewed the documents received through the night and scanned through his emails. The PMO worked *24*7*. Looking through the large windows that overlooked the Rashtrapati Bhawan, he took a moment to take in its breath-taking splendour. He wished for more of such times post the elections. There was a knock at his door and Goswami came in, five minutes before the meeting was scheduled to commence.

'How is Adhikari? He must be shaken,' Goswami politely asked.

'Naturally... but he is a strong leader.' Doshi answered.

'If you don't mind, may I...?' Goswami said, and looked behind to check if the door was still closed.

'Go ahead, by all means.'

'Sir, we all know Adhikari was strong because of Raut and Pawar. Together, they were a formidable team... alone, he is vulnerable. Do you want to consider another candidate? It's not too late yet,' Goswami suggested.

'I unxderstand your concern, Goswami. But I am confident that Sanjay will make a good prime minister,' Doshi said with a finality, and gestured towards the exit. It was time for the meeting.

Is he hinting at himself to be the other candidate? Could Goswami, with his access to information and the connections to pass it on to, be the traitor? Doshi wondered.

The stubborn, old man is hell bent on sacrificing Adhikari. Nothing could save him now, Goswami concluded.

Both men shook their heads lightly, and walked in silence as they made their way down the corridor of the twenty-room PMO.

***

The PMO was equipped to provide both infrastructural and manpower support to the nation's chief executive, including hi-tech accessories and sophisticated communication devices to monitor domestic and international developments.

They entered a conference room adjacent to the defence ministry. The entire central team was already seated inside, and they smiled and greeted the prime minister respectfully as he sat down at his usual place. Doshi acknowledged them with folded hands, and looked around the roomful of his colleagues and friends; all of them trusted aides for years. And yet, because of one of them, the love and respect was now replaced with bitterness and hate, and suspicion for all of them. He wondered which one of them would break his heart. But that's what politics was all about – lies are told, trusts are broken. And Doshi had been in the game long enough to know it better than anyone. For the first time in his conscious memory, he viewed each one of them through a different lens. He was determined to find out who it was before it was too late.

As they went through the agenda, Doshi was unable to shake off the notion that there was a traitor amongst them. He became more focused on observing the people around him, than the issues that were being discussed.

Devika has been unusually silent and withdrawn of late, he thought, *especially after the announcement at Davos. I hope that the decision to field Adhikari as the prime minister isn't the reason for her changed behaviour. Ambition is a virtue, but not before time. And Devika is not foolish enough to aspire for the top job so soon. It is probably something to do with Rajan.*

He never did like the man; he was someone who could have done anything to gain power.

'We need a formal plan to deliver connected welfare,' Jha thumped the table. The discussion had veered towards the theme of Human Centricity, a theme pioneered by Doshi, to develop better synergies between national and local welfare organizations. The disconnect between the two was proving to be costly and inefficient for the nation, and disheartening for the individual.

'I agree... and there is also a need to integrate employment in the welfare ecosystem,' Goswami added.

'The question is – will that make the program unmanageable?' Jha said. 'And importantly, will we derive its benefit in time for the elections?' Other members joined the debate, but were careful when making a point against Jha's stand. Doshi knew the power Jha commanded, and it had been a tough decision not to give the top post to him.

Jha had been visibly – and vocally – upset with Doshi's decision. He had confronted him shortly after the announcement in Davos. *Why have I been overlooked for the job? Jha had demanded to know.* And while Doshi had tried to explain his rationale to Jha, at the end of their long conversation, Jha had simply shrugged it off. *'It's your choice...it does not matter whether I am happy or not... but you have my full support,'* was all he had said.

And after that day, while Jha had never brought up the topic again, Doshi was not sure if he had managed to convince him. Jha certainly had it in him to be ruthless, as Doshi had discovered in his first tenure as the chief minister of Gujarat. But if Doshi had anyone he considered family; it was Jha. He shook his head and let out a deep sigh. It couldn't be Jha; he was not capable of stabbing him in the back.

'You are unusually preoccupied today,' Mahajan commented, as he walked out of the conference room with Doshi. While Mahajan did not hold any portfolio officially, he was always present in committee meetings, especially those chaired by Doshi. That day, Mahajan was also present in Doshi's thoughts as he traced their history together. Doshi was inducted in the IPP a few years after Mahajan. Both considered to be promising leaders by the then party leadership. They both had thrown their hats in the ring for the post of the party's general secretary, which Doshi had won by the proverbial whisker. Though initially upset, Mahajan accepted the party's decision gracefully. Since then, he played a strong supporting and advisor role in the IPP, with the party relying on his wisdom and political acumen as it continued to emerge as the strongest national party in the country.

'Yes, just a little tired,' Doshi said, leading his senior colleague and friend to his office. 'What do you make of the current situation?' he asked.

'Well, for one, Sanjay should avoid too many public appearances until the elections are over. We have practically won; the sympathy factor will only strengthen our position.'

Doshi nodded in agreement; Mahajan was right in his assessment. Doshi wondered if, given the current circumstances, the party would have done better by choosing Mahajan over him. Mahajan, too, had the ambition. And while the wound was old, was it deep enough?

'More importantly,' Mahajan continued, 'we have to be prepared for the worst-case scenario. In case something were to happen to Sanjay, you'll have to take back your resignation. The party... and the country... will need that.'

But Doshi knew he would not continue. He couldn't, even if he wanted to. He did not have a choice, or the time.

34

Tamas drove the car away from St. Xavier's college, driving well within the speed limit. In the opposite lane, two police vans sped towards the college. M removed her grey wig and dumped it in a plastic bag. As she started to unbutton the grey shirt of her uniform, she caught Tamas staring at her. He shifted his attention back to the road when he saw the light blue shirt she had worn underneath.

'Stop the car here. There is a police blockade ahead,' M told him, pointing to the heavy traffic that was building up in front of them. M got down from the Wagon-R. Tamas signaled an apology to the honking vehicles behind him, and inched the car towards the Crawford Market junction.

The Indian police possesses wide discretionary powers of stop and search. One regular manifestation of this power is a blockade, referred to as a *nakabandi,* where the police set up road blocks at important road junctions. Being a common site on Mumbai roads, police nakabandi did not raise any controversies like it could have in the West. However, several questions regarding its purpose and efficacy arose, especially in relation to the amount of time and resources devoted to these operations. That day, however, the blockade at the Crawford Market junction did not raise any questions from a majority of the motorists who, by now, knew about the assassination of Gautam Pawar.

Sub-inspector Barve and his team inspected each vehicle and its occupants as they passed through the blockade. Generally, they would be on the lookout for a specific car or person, but today, the police didn't have any leads. It was standard protocol after an incident of this nature. At random, Barve stopped an SUV and checked the license of the driver, asking him a few questions.

Where was he coming from? Where was he headed? Two cars behind, a bead of sweat appeared on Tamas' forehead; he put on his sunglasses. The inspector waved the car in front through without stopping it; Tamas hoped to get the same treatment. But the inspector put his palm up, and asked him to pull over. Tamas felt a sudden discomfort rising in his chest. He felt the urge to get out from the car and run away.

Barve leaned in through the window on the passenger side. 'License please,' he said, in an authoritative tone. Tamas took out a worn-out leather wallet from the glove compartment and handed over his driving license into the outstretched hand of the cop. Barve looked at the faded photograph on the card. *Vinay Kamath.* He gestured to the driver to remove his dark glasses. Tamas, his hands shaking, removed the sun glasses, and managed a weak smile.

'Are you alright?' Barve asked the sweating man.

'Yes, sir, absolutely fine,' Tamas replied, trying to sound calm.

Barve looked intently at him for a moment, when his phone rang. It was headquarters. He signalled the car to go through, and walked back to the kerb to answer the phone. But there was something about the man that bothered him; he had seen that face before. He made a mental note of the car's number plate.

35

Chen Jintao was due to meet a diplomatic delegation from Angola in an hour. Under the guise of economic progress promised by the BRI, Jintao was the chief architect of China's debt-trap diplomacy. Angola was the most leveraged African nation, with borrowings of more than thirty billion dollars from China. The cash-strapped nation, in a last-ditch attempt, had sent a senior delegation to meet Jintao to try and renegotiate the terms of the contract. Jintao was in no mood to show any leniency, but he liked to see powerful leaders imploring to him for repayment extensions or a change of terms; some even broke down in front of him. It made him feel powerful. He looked forward to the meeting.

When in office, he preferred a working lunch. His secretary of more than a decade, Fang Tiwu, made her way into Jintao's spacious cabin as the clock struck 1 and served her boss his standard fare of *gaifan*.

There was a knock at the door, and Hong Lin peeped in. Jintao asked him to come in, and dug into his meal as his two subordinates sat down across from him. Lin smiled at Fang, and shuffled in his seat. A gigantic portrait of Xi Liu, hung on the red wall directly behind Jintao's desk, stared down menacingly at them. It never failed to intimidate Lin.

Jintao was running out of time; he *had* to find the mole in his camp. He had narrowed down his suspicion to the two people seated in front of him. Both of them had access to his office, and could have overheard his conversations with the Serpent. Had he slipped up? Although he was certain that possibility was almost nil. He had replayed in his mind all the times he had had a discussion with, or about, the Serpent or the India operation; and he could not think of anyone else in his circle who could be the leak. *It has to be one of these two,* he had concluded.

He could sense the unease in the room as he quietly ate his lunch, looking at Lin and Fang from time to time.

As both Lin and Fang waited with open diaries and pens ready for Jintao's instructions, he switched on the television mounted on the wall to his right. He surfed through a couple of channels and settled in on CGTN, where a business journalist was summarizing China's economic resilience in a tough economic time across the world. Jintao soon lost interest and focused on his meal instead. But after a few minutes, a segment in the World News caught his attention. The story being covered was the second assassination, in quick succession, of two rising Indian political stars. The news coverage showed footage of the scene of the crime, where Gautam Pawar, a leader of the ruling party, was killed. Jintao's eyes widened as the Serpent came on the television screen. The Serpent expressed his shock and anger at the two killings, and condemned terrorism. He ended his press briefing by promising to bring to justice the people behind the barbaric acts.

Jintao smiled and shook his head, his mood suddenly brighter. 'One step closer,' he muttered under his breath. Lin stared at the face on the television screen. It was the face of the man he had seen with Jintao at Khorgos. And suddenly, all the pieces of the jigsaw puzzle fell into place. He did not have to worry about finding the identity of the woman anymore; he had just discovered something infinitely better.

36

Fang Tiwu finished cleaning up after dinner and settled down on a sofa in the living room of her one-bedroom apartment. She was exhausted; it was almost 10 p.m. and she needed a few hours of shut-eye before the next day began. The last few months had been especially tiring at work, and she felt completely drained out, both mentally and physically. She did not remember the last time she had taken a vacation, not that she could afford one with her current finances.

'Good night, mama,' her teenage daughter called out as she switched off the lights in the bedroom.

The thin woman walked up to her only child and kissed her on the cheeks. 'Good night, darling,' she whispered. She closed the door behind her and resumed work on the last of the documents Jintao had asked her to proof-read. It was another half an hour before she sank fully clothed into bed. Ten minutes later, as she was about to fall asleep, her phone pinged.

Her eyes widened when she read the SMS from her bank. *CNY 6,50,000 has been credited to your account 002XXXXXX001. Your available balance is CNY 6,62,000.* It was surely a mistake. The amount was more than five times her annual salary. She stepped out of the bedroom and called the customer care number of the bank to inform them of the error, but a pre-recorded message played, asking customers to call during working hours. Fang's heart was thumping out of her chest; she decided to visit the bank first thing in the morning and get the matter sorted out at the earliest.

***

The next morning, Fang Tiwu was at the entrance of the Bank of

China's Jinsong branch, where she had her account, a little before opening hours. As the shutters opened, she rushed in, clutching her phone in one hand, and a purse in another. The staff at the help desk guided her to a waiting area, as the tellers and the service officers finished their morning huddle with the branch manager and walked towards their desks.

A few minutes later, a young officer gestured to Fang, calling her over. Before Fang could get up, she was accosted by two men in dark suits. 'Ms Fang Tiwu, you are required to come with us,' one of them said plainly.

'But... who are you?'

'MSS. Now please, shall we?' the man nudged her elbow. Fang's breath quickened; her eyes started to water and sweat trickled down her neck. A few staff, including the branch manager, had started to gather around them.

'I was here to...,' she held out her phone with trembling hands. Neither of the men responded. A sobbing Fang Tiwu was led into a waiting car. As the car drove away, she stared out of the window as Beijing was coming to life on a sunny Saturday morning. She thought of her daughter and what would become of her, when she felt the needle jab into her neck.

***

Chen Jintao was disappointed. He was very fond of Fang. *And he could still not fathom that she had betrayed him.* Over the past several days, at his behest, the Ministry of State Security (MSS), or *Guoanbu*, was keeping a close watch over Fang and Lin. The surveillance was not restricted to a team on a stakeout for the two suspects, but also a detailed scrutiny of their bank statements, phone records, past travels. Keeping a tab on their close family was not difficult for the MSS; Fang was a single mother, bereaved a few years back, with hardly any social life. Lin stayed alone; his parents had moved back to their village in Yihezhuang.

Jintao was almost certain it would turn out to be Lin. He had known Fang for many years; she was a God-fearing, conscientious woman. *Or at least, he had thought so until now.* As soon as the funds were credited to Fang's account, the MSS had been notified. On following the money trail, the MSS had traced the origin to India. Jintao's orders to the MSS were unambiguous. There was only one way out for traitors.

Jintao couldn't help but smile when he called the Serpent to deliver the good news.

***

Hong Lin was tense as he made his way through Beihai park that Saturday evening. He could see people walking, children playing; but he could not hear anything because of the blood rushing in his ears. The air around him was so brittle that he felt it could snap. He tried to calm himself down. He had been trying to do so for over a day. *Today is the last time. After I deliver this one name, I have more than repaid what I owed the Indian. No more fear. No more looking over my shoulder all the time.* Lin intended to convey this in no uncertain terms to the Indian.

The bench was empty. Lin sat down, and looked around. He removed the sealed paper pouch, no longer than his index finger, from the pocket of his shirt. Staring directly in front of him, motionless except for his left hand, he stuck the sachet beneath the plank of the seat at its left edge. He sat there for a few minutes, before starting his walk back.

Lin could feel the fear in his chest evaporating into thin air. Perhaps it had been there earlier only to protect him, to ensure he was being cautious; there was really no danger. He decided to treat himself to a celebratory dinner that evening. He was finally free.

***

A man, dressed in running gear, jogged off the track towards the bench that Lin had just vacated and sat down on it. He found nothing unusual about a man going for a walk in the park every Saturday. But sitting alone at the same place, and not the most scenic one at that, was the part of Lin's ritual that he had found strange. There was nothing on the bench. The MSS agent, his brows creased, sat slumped; he just couldn't shake the intuition that came with fifteen years of field-work. After five long minutes, he shook his head and got up. When he was a few paces away, a young boy, less than four years old, came running towards the bench. He giggled, waved his tiny arms towards his mother, who was a few paces behind him, and slid under the bench. The child squealed with delight as his mother discovered his 'hiding place' and scooped him up. The MSS man smiled at the woman as she passed him, and then retraced his steps back to the bench. He knelt down and looked underneath the wooden planks.

***

Had the MSS been as efficient as they normally were, Hong Lin would not have been caught. The news of Fang Tiwu's arrest that morning had not been communicated to the agents who were assigned to keep a tab on Lin. As a result, they continued their surveillance and followed Lin to Beihai park that Saturday evening.

For the first time ever, it was an incompetency that Jintao pardoned. The only regret he had was that Fang had been eliminated needlessly. He realized that the money would have been deposited in Fang's account by the person from India who 'ran' Lin, in an obvious attempt to divert attention away from Lin – the *real* traitor. Jintao wanted to deal with this situation personally. He wanted to send a fitting message to the Indians. He, once again, looked at the piece of paper hidden in the pouch that Hong Lin had tried to deliver to India. Jintao slumped in his chair with relief as he read the note; it would have been catastrophic if it had been delivered. *The Serpent's name was written on it.*

***

Hong Lin lay sprawled on a bench in Beihai park. His eyes were open, vacantly and fixedly staring at the skies. His hair fluttered in the morning breeze; the rest of him lay utterly still. As the footfalls of the morning walkers approached, crunching the gravel, a cursory glance was enough for them to know he was dead.

37

'What is the progress?' Adhikari asked.

'Sir, we are doing everything we can,' Anant said.

Adhikari had called for a meeting with Sarathi and Anant at his residence to review the terror situation and how close the ATS was in apprehending the killer. It had been a week since Pawar's death, and the city was still on high alert.

'I know, Anant, you don't have to justify anything to me,' Adhikari reassured the two cops.

It was his unstinting faith in the ATS and the police force, especially in such trying times, that had earned Adhikari their respect. He had the rare quality to not make everything a political issue, allowing each department in his administration to perform at its best. Anant felt that while Adhikari looked visibly tired, there was grit written over his face.

'Sir, can we go over your itinerary for the next few weeks?' Anant asked.

'Sure,' Adhikari pressed a button on his intercom to summon Dalvi. The chief minister's head of security walked in within a minute, carrying a dossier. He passed a copy of Adhikari's schedule to Anant and Sarathi.

'I am not cancelling any of those... I have advised that to the prime minister as well.' Adhikari smiled, pre-empting the suggestion he knew would be coming.

'I have known you for many years, sir. I would expect nothing less,' Sarathi said.

Anant was engrossed in the list. Most of the meetings on Adhikari's schedule were with various lobbies and trade bodies, which were planned to be held behind closed doors. He put a neat blue tick against them; they would be relatively easier to control and monitor. The chief minister had planned two more public rallies as a part of the final leg of his campaign. Anant frowned; they will have to significantly enhance the protection cover during those.

'Sir, for these two rallies,' Anant pointed to the two public events, 'we have to further beef up the security arrangements. I suggest we take assistance from the CRPF[3].'

Adhikari was uncertain if he wanted to call up Namit Jha for help. After deliberating for a few seconds, he decided he would route his request through Doshi. 'Okay, I can arrange for that,' he said, looking at Dalvi, who nodded.

'Thank you,' Anant said.

At least the two events were at familiar public places. He knew the two locations and the encircling vantage points like the back of his hand. But his gaze was fixed on 30 June in Adhikari's schedule. He circled the event and underlined it. That was the one that really worried him.

30th June.

The Sethna Mumbai Marathon.

The prime minister.

The chief minister.

More than 60,000 people.

And the inauguration of the Mumbai Coastal Road – hitherto a completely unknown terrain.

***

'I should be there in ten minutes. Hope you're ready,' Anant told Nandini on the phone.

He was driving back after a tense, but largely uneventful day at work. Adhikari had addressed a public rally at Shivaji Park – his

---

[3] The Central Reserve Police Force (CRPF), which functioned under the authority of the union home minister, is the premier central police force in India for internal security and counter-insurgency.

first appearance in front of a large gathering after Pawar's killing. The entire police force was on the edge, and save for a few minor turf issues with the CRPF, the day passed by peacefully enough.

After a short detour, Anant reached home and rang the doorbell. 'I am ready,' Nandini said as she opened the door. She was wearing a black salwar-kameez, which now hung loose on her once healthy figure. Anant's heart skipped a beat. There was something in her dark brown eyes that was so beautiful and warm. He hugged her, never wanting to let go.

'Happy fifteenth anniversary,' Anant whispered in Nandini's ears.

'So, you remembered?'

'Of course, I always do.'

'Remember our ninth anniversary?' Nandini laughed. It was a joke they shared; Anant had forgotten their anniversary that once. But later, whenever Nandini spoke about it, he claimed to have remembered it all along.

'These are for you,' Anant gave her a bunch of red roses he had picked up on his way back.

'Thank you,' she kissed him, and set the flowers in a vase on the centre-table. She had made a dinner reservation at their favourite restaurant. It was where they had gone on their first date. She wanted to make the day memorable for Anant; she was sure this was the last anniversary they were celebrating together.

'This place hasn't changed a bit,' Nandini said as they entered the restaurant.

'Neither have you,' Anant winked at her, as they were led to their reserved table.

Anant ordered a Reisling for Nandini, and a fresh juice for himself. He filled her in on the day's highlights, as he normally did. 'By the way, you remember Ryan?' Anant asked.

'Of course, I do! How is he doing?' Nandini asked. Anant had told her all about the little boy, and how he had had a narrow escape from the clutches of an almost certain death. *Thanks to the man sitting across from her,* she thought.

'He has recovered fully,' Anant reassured her. 'In fact, he returned to the shelter today. The NGO that has taken over the facility made the arrangements for his transfer. Rego confirmed that he has reached Goa safely, and is happy to be reunited with his friends.'

'Thank god for that. Does he remember anything that could help the case?'

'Nothing, unfortunately. He was playing with a few kids; does not recall anything after that,' Anant shook his head.

'I can understand. He is alive and well – hope his life gets better.'

'Amen to that,' Anant clinked his glass with hers. Just then, his phone rang. Anant looked at the caller-id and hesitated for a moment. He mouthed a 'sorry' to Nandini, who smiled and encouraged him to answer the call.

'Barve, how are you?' Anant answered. It had been more than a year since he had last spoken with the sub-inspector.

'Sir, it may be nothing, but I thought it was best to bring it to your notice,' Barve said.

'Go on, Barve. I am listening,' Anant leaned forward on the table.

'The day Pawar saheb was killed, I was at a nakabandi at Crawford Market. We stopped a car... I had a vague sense of familiarity when I saw the driver... who I could not place at the time, but I have been racking my brain ever since... and... and suddenly today, I recognised the face... it was Tamas, sir.'

Barve continued, 'He may have nothing to do with the case, but him being in the vicinity... and he had shown me a fake license.... I thought it was better to bring it to your attention, in case it helps,' Barve said.

'Thank you, Barve. Which direction was he coming from?' Anant asked.

'Sir, he was coming from CST junction. I also noted down the car number.'

Anant thanked Barve and hung up. Tamas. He was a fixer; a go-to man for criminals. He had served time for his involvement in an extortion racket and was once caught in possession of illegal arms. *What was he doing there? Was he involved somehow?* It was too much of a coincidence for Anant to ignore. And who knew? Maybe it could be the first solid lead in the case.

38

After dinner, Anant dropped Nandini home, apologising for cutting their evening short, and went back to his office. He had already messaged his team, including sub-inspector Barve, to assemble for a briefing. Given the current situation, they couldn't spare a single second. The future of the country was at stake. He knew he had to strike a fine balance when allocating resources in his hunt for Tamas. If it turned out to be a wild goose chase, it would not only be an effort wasted, but further increase the chances of the killer's ultimate mission being successful.

Anant gathered his team in the conference room and gave them a brief update. He invited Barve to recount his run-in with Tamas. He, too, wanted to hear it from him in person. A few of the cops present nodded knowingly when Tamas' name cropped up. Anant signalled to Ashraf, who opened a police file he had brought along. Pinned on the first page was a postcard sized photograph of Tamas. He clicked a picture of the photo with his phone, and with the help of the presentation equipment in the room, projected the picture on the white screen.

A pudgy, childlike face with spectacles stared back at the roomful of cops. 'It's him... the man I saw,' Barve gesticulated in excitement.

Anant was waiting for one more piece of information before he gave out instructions to the troops. After a few minutes, Anant's phone buzzed; he grabbed it at the first ring. 'Thanks a lot,' he hung up the phone and looked at his messages. He clicked on the one he had just received. It was a video. He hit the play button on his phone and shared his screen. The big, white screen lit up with the grainy closed-circuit video footage of the CST junction.

The time on the top right corner indicated it was just before 11 a.m. on 02 June, the day Pawar was killed at St. Xavier's college. The scene at the junction was like any other regular day – traffic flowing from all directions, albeit lesser than working days. Anant fast-forwarded the video to the point where a horde of people emerged from the left side of the screen – from the street where the college was. Soon, the crowds began to swell. There was chaos on the screen; each person for themselves, fear written all over their faces.

Anant waited. A few minutes later, a Wagon-R emerged from the bottom left corner of the screen. It eased forward slowly until it reached the main junction, where it stopped just after the traffic lights. A curly-haired man was at the wheel. He was alone in the car. 'That's him... that's the car,' yelled Barve. Sixteen eyes stared at the screen without blinking. As the car had moved ahead, Barve leaned forward and confirmed the car number, nodding feverishly. Nothing seemed to happen for some time. Anant grimaced as the scrambling crowd around the car obstructed a clear vision of it. The mass of people had a life of its own now – dragged in both directions, towards and away from the scene of the crime.

And then, in a flash, the car door on the passenger side in the front opened, and someone got in. Almost immediately, the car pulled away. In seconds, it had disappeared out of view from the top of the screen. Anant rewound the video, carefully sliding his index finger on the phone's screen. He paused the playback at the point when the car door was opened by someone.

He frowned because he could not get a clearer view of the scene. People, all of them wearing a serious expression, swirled around the car as if it was a barricade. Anant pinched the screen on his phone and zoomed in as much as he could. The image was a grainy collage of blacks and whites, with dots and lines scratching the screen. But, at last, Anant could clearly make out the coarse figure of a woman getting into the car.

39

Prabhat deftly navigated his bike through the congested lane near Dadar station. A serpentine queue of *kaali-peeli* cabs had formed right outside the station, awaiting outstation passengers, who flooded the street every time a train arrived at the platform. On Sunday night, it was relatively less busy; on other days, the area overflowed with office-goers. But, for Prabhat, weekends were busier. He preferred not to come to this area – finding a parking spot, even for a bike, was difficult. But he had no choice in the matter.

Prabhat neared his destination – Hotel Shapoor. As usual, the restaurant was packed; there were more customers jostling on the pavement, waiting for takeaways, than those seated inside. He revved his bike as he spotted an opening a few metres ahead of the restaurant, and manoeuvred his bike between the two parked scooters. He took off his helmet and walked to the restaurant counter. His black tee stuck to his body. The weather in Mumbai was oppressive; it was mid-June and still, there were no signs of rain. The old man at the counter of the restaurant recognized Prabhat and waved to him. He then barked to the sweating man in the kitchen, 'F2D's order is ready?'. 'Two minutes,' he gestured to Prabhat.

Things were finally looking up for Prabhat. A year ago, he had lost his job, as the travel company he was working with shut down. Inspite of trying hard, he could not find another job. He even postponed his wedding until he was settled. Finally, six months ago, he got a job with Food-2-Door, or F2D as it was popularly known. The food delivery business was picking up; people were eating out and ordering more, almost as if with a vengeance. He had been on the field since morning, as was usual on weekends. Thankfully, it was his last pickup before he called it a day.

He collected the food container and checked the delivery address on his phone. He knew the location well. He slid his bike out of parking, and made his way through the heavy traffic. He reached his destination within twenty minutes, parked his bike in the compound of the housing complex and checked his phone for the wing and flat number. An old security guard was sitting in the lobby with an open register at his desk. Prabhat walked up to him and took out the food container.

'You will have to go up and deliver it yourself,' the guard said. Prabhat gave him a puzzled look.

'The intercom is not working,' the old man clarified. Prabhat entered his name and phone number in the register, and while doing so, confirmed with the guard the floor he had to go to. Once inside the lift, he pressed the button for his destination floor and looked at himself in the full-length mirror. Keeping the food container on the floor, he quickly combed his hair. As the lift doors opened, he saw that the flat was directly opposite. Prabhat rang the doorbell and waited. Nobody answered the door. He rang the bell again. 'Coming,' a voice shouted from inside, and Prabhat heard footsteps approaching the door from the other side.

After a few seconds, Tamas opened the door.

***

Two years ago, a very private conversation had taken place between Anant and Sarathi. With more than 180 terrorist groups operating within India over the last two decades, with their networks operating in or from neighbouring countries such as Nepal, Bangladesh or Pakistan, the ATS had decided to develop a new strategy to recruit informants. Anant wanted as many eyes and ears as possible to acquire on-ground intelligence, that would otherwise take the ATS years to procure, if at all. All information would be controlled and disseminated by a small team, reporting directly to Anant. Sarathi had promised to get the 'informal budget' approved by the chief minister. The network would have to be suitably rewarded, after all; counting solely on their patriotism would not get them far.

Anant had zeroed in on two networks. One, the ridesharing or the taxi-on-call service; and second, the food delivery service. Between the two new businesses, they had recruited upwards of three million employees across the length and breadth of the country in the last two years. For the ATS, this was a golden opportunity, if used well. Of course, the ATS could not advertise their offer, and hence, the network was formed incrementally over time. With a stringent screening and selection process of the individual before 'recruitment', the active informant network was now more than 300,000 across India.

The information coming from the 'network' had to be sifted carefully and quickly. A set of informants was assigned to every officer of the ATS, including Anant. The description of the suspect, and at times, a picture, if one was available, was sent to the phones of the informants; no other information was provided. If there was a match, or even the hint of a suspicion, the network members simply called their handlers, and handed over the information. *Snippets of conversation. A name. A place. A date. Pickup and drop-off address.* There were many false positives, but the back-end team, with their sophisticated systems, was able to screen and filter information to reduce these to a manageable number for the ATS and the police force.

When there was no evidence of a planned operation by the suspects, Anant had used a catch-and-release program for suspected terror operatives. The suspect would be caught and kept under custody for a few hours or a couple of days at the most, and then released. This created reluctance or fear in such suspects and prevented them from further acts or, perhaps more important, created distrust in the cell leaders of these individuals in the future.

Prabhat was fervent about his new voluntary responsibility. It also added a sense of thrill to his otherwise mundane job. Each delivery was now an adventure. As Prabhat looked at the short, curly-haired man who opened the door, there was a familiarity to his face that he could not shake. He handed over the food packet and the bill into the outstretched hand of his customer.

'Wait, I'll get the cash,' Tamas told him, glancing at the bill.

With his heart-rate accelerating, Prabhat opened the chat application on his phone and clicked on the last message he had received from Kulkarni Sir. His eyes popped as he looked at the picture he had received a few days back. Important – the caption highlighted. It was the same man; the customer at whose doorstep he was now standing. Prabhat had no doubt in his mind. He was still looking at his phone when the man in the picture reappeared at the door.

'Here you go, keep the change,' Tamas said, handing two five-hundred-rupee notes to Prabhat, who was shuffling his feet. Tamas glimpsed an expression of recognition in the delivery boy's eyes for only a fraction of a second, but it was enough for him to catch it.

'Thank you, sir,' Prabhat turned, and pressed the button on the elevator panel. He was in a hurry to escape and send the information ahead to Kulkarni sir. As the elevator doors opened, he stepped inside, and started to type a reply to the message from Anant. In the mirror, he saw the man in the picture looming towards him.

40

M parked the Wagon-R and rode the elevator up. She was exhausted, and looked forward to a hot shower and a good night's sleep. As she opened the door to the apartment, she sensed something was wrong. Instinctively, she drew out her pistol from her handbag, and went towards the bedrooms; her room was locked, the way she had left it. With her toes, she pushed open the door to the other bedroom.

A young man, in his late twenties, lay still on the ground. There was blood on his face and neck. Tamas was sitting beside the body on the floor. There were scratch marks on his forearms, and blood on his knuckles.

'What happened here?' she asked. Tamas told her the events that had taken place that evening.

'And how do you think he recognized you?' M asked. Tamas shrugged his shoulders. M took out the dead man's phone from his pocket. It was locked. She lifted the man's right hand and placed his index finger on the home button. *No luck.* She did the same with his left hand. The screen lit up in green.

She looked at his phone history. There were no calls made or received since he had come there to deliver the food. She opened his chat box, and her expression changed.

'Clear out the place – we have to leave,' she ordered, taking in a deep, even breath.

'But... what... why?' Tamas protested.

'Now,' M fixed him with an icy stare. Tamas nodded, and scrambled out of the room. She removed the battery from the phone and smashed the device, as well as the battery. She wanted to ensure that tracking the phone became as difficult as possible.

She went to her room and shoved her minimal belongings

in a travel bag. Her backpack was already packed with her 'professional' equipment, kept ready in case she had to make a quick escape.

'Where is Bandhu?' she asked Tamas, as he stepped out of his room with a bag in his hands.

'He has gone out for a run.'

'Have you checked and cleaned out all the rooms?'

'Yes, all done. Let's go,' Tamas said, and started to walk towards the main door.

'You're staying here,' M said. As Tamas turned around, with a puzzled look on his face, M fired the gun.

***

Anant tucked Nandini in, and waited by her bedside, watching her fall asleep.

As he stood there, his phone pinged. He grew excited when he saw it was a message from Prabhat, one of his informants. *A reply to Tamas' photograph he had broadcast to his network of informants.* He was disappointed when he saw the message contained only the word – *'Sir, he'*. At once, Anant dialled Prabhat's number. The phone was switched off. He kept trying the number as he put his gun in its holster and slipped on his shoes. 'Damn it,' he shouted out aloud as the response remained the same. He was sure Prabhat had some useful information, but was unable to send it for some reason. *Is he in trouble?*

'I am sending you a number. Get me the last known location,' Anant called the cybercrime cell as he rushed down and started his car. He sat inside the car, got the engine running, and waited.

He texted Prabhat's phone number to Ashraf, and called him up. 'Ashraf, we may have something. Call F2D and find out the addresses where Prabhat made deliveries between nine and ten tonight... also the restaurants he picked up food from in this time period. Get ready, we may finally have something.'

41

'What have you got?' Anant picked up the phone at the first ring. It was the cybercrime cell.

'Sir, we will need some more time. The battery is either dead or removed,' the caller informed Anant. He cursed under his breath, and slammed his hands on the steering wheel. Almost immediately, his phone rang again. It was Ashraf.

'Sir, got the details from F2D. Prabhat's last delivery was to 1803, Centrum Residency, Wadala, at 9:40 p.m. He picked up the food from Hotel Shapoor, near Dadar station, at 9:20.'

Anant thought about the information he had at hand; the incomplete message from Prabhat was received by Anant at 9:44 p.m. *Right after he must have delivered the food.* So, chances were he spotted Tamas at the tower. Of course, he may have seen him somewhere else, on another day, and remembered to inform him today; or it was a case of mistaken identity. But he decided it was worth exploring.

'Excellent. I am on my way to Wadala. Get there with the team as soon as you can,' he told Ashraf.

'I am already on my way, sir.'

Anant rarely used the police siren on his car, but that night, he turned on both, the lights and the siren, and raced towards his destination. If it was indeed Tamas, and the woman, who were at the place he was heading towards, they had been less than three kilometres from his house. He shook his head in disbelief. He covered the short distance in under ten minutes. The guard at the building's entrance stood up in attention as Anant walked past him and stepped inside the elevator.

He took out his gun from the holster and checked it; it was fully loaded. He wasn't going to make the same mistake he made with Omkar. He rang the bell of flat number 1803 and waited, looking up at the camera in the lobby. When there was no answer, he aimed at the body of the lock, above the latch, and fired. The silence was broken by the sound of the gunshot. He knew what the repercussions would be if it was a false alarm, but he would deal with them later, if he had to. Anant kicked open the door, and waited for a few seconds before he stepped inside the flat. There was complete darkness in the house. Gun drawn, Anant switched on the torch of his mobile phone and scanned the room. He saw the switchboard, and turned on the lights. A very dead Tamas lay on his back, a few feet away from the door, in a pool of blood. His curly hair was stained with fresh blood; his eyes were still wide open, staring in surprise through the crooked glasses. A travel bag lay beside him, as if his escape had been interrupted by the bullet that had pierced his heart.

Anant let out a hoarse cry when he discovered Prabhat's body in the bedroom. He felt responsible for him, as with all his informants, and this was the first time he had lost someone in the network. He knelt down by the young man and offered a silent prayer. And an apology.

42

Bandhu completed his speed run that evening; his last before the marathon next week. He wanted to dedicate the coming week to fine-tune his plan for the mission, including a recce at the actual location. Then all he had to do was execute the plan. The beauty of the plan lay in its simplicity, and he was sure he could pull it off easily. Cooling down, he was jogging at a slow pace towards the apartment building, and was less than a block away, when he saw a police car, sirens blaring, entering the compound. He made a U-turn, upped his pace, and continued running. He looked up only after he was a safe distance away, and took out his phone. There were six missed calls from M.

'Where have you been? Don't go anywhere near the apartment,' M told him when he called her.

'Yeah... I saw... the cops are here... what happened?' Bandhu asked.

M filled him in on what had taken place at the apartment. 'And Tamas?' Bandhu asked.

'He had become a liability. Cops were looking for him; we cannot take a risk like that. Anyway, I am texting you an address... come there,' M replied plainly.

Bandhu remained silent, anger welling up inside him. *You bitch, you killed my friend. I can't wait to slit your throat.* But for that, he decided to wait until the mission was over; he had worked hard on it, and he did not want to let go of the reward at the end of it.

***

'Who all stay in 1803?' Anant asked the security guard. Ashraf was at the apartment with a team of cops and the forensics unit.

As news of the murders spread, a couple of residents were down in the lobby, having an animated conversation with one another. A few others were peeping below from their windows; most of the other flats, unoccupied, lay in darkness.

'Two men... and a woman,' the security guard replied.

'*Two* men? Are you sure?' Anant asked.

'Yes, sir... I am quite sure. The woman left in their car just before you arrived, sir.'

'Can you tell me something more about her? How did she look?' Anant asked desperately. 'Or the other man... not this one?' Anant showed Tamas' picture on his phone.

'I don't have any details about them, sir. And I have seen her... and the men... only a couple of times... that, too, just a glimpse... difficult to describe her, sir... the man had a beard – that's all I can say,' the guard stuttered. *That's not much help, Anant frowned.*

'What about that camera?' Anant pointed to the CCTV camera in the lobby.

'That does not work, sir,' a resident standing nearby had overheard the conversation and had walked over to Anant. 'We have complained to the society a few times, but to no avail.'

Anant sighed in frustration; he had narrowly missed her. The rest of the discussion with the guard and the residents did not yield any more useful information. Nobody seemed to know them, and they had never interacted with anyone else. They were assumed to be new tenants in an otherwise unoccupied flat. Nobody had met the owner of the flat either.

'Anything?' Anant asked Ashraf, who had joined him after a thorough sweep of the apartment.

'Nothing so far, the forensics team is still there... so let's see if we get something in a few days,' Ashraf said, shaking his head.

'It might be too late... we have less than a week. You be around here for some time, the other man may return, though I am pretty sure he has been alerted already.'

***

It was a lucky escape today, M thought. She was another faceless commuter, when she got down from the local train at CST that night. She stepped out on the main road, just across from where, a few days back, she had carried out the audacious assassination of Pawar. *Fond memories.*

The black SUV was waiting at the exact spot that the Serpent had mentioned. As she got into it, the driver drove off without a word. *Coming Sunday, by this time, everything would be over; and she would be in another country.* M couldn't wait.

43

The bell rang exactly at noon, marking the end of the school day. Within minutes, children came running out, much brighter and buoyant than when they had gone in a few hours ago. Naima bade goodbye to her best friend, and waited for Ammi to arrive.

'Abbu,' she jumped with joy when she instead saw Ashraf walking in through the gate. She jumped into his outstretched arms; he lobbed her playfully in the air and hugged her tight. Naima's words ran into one another and Ashraf had no clue what she was saying in her obvious excitement. He laughed in delight.

The team had worked without a break for the last few days, and at Anant's insistence, Ashraf had taken the afternoon off. He could not recollect the last time he had picked up Naima from her school.

The first time he had visited the school was with Faiza, his estranged wife. More than two years back, they had come to the school together for the parents' interview as a part of the application process for Naima's admission. Soon after, Faiza had left him for her wealthy lover. Her sudden decision had devastated Ashraf. He tried, desperately, to convince her to come back. For Naima's sake, if not his. But she did not relent, and went away, leaving Ashraf heartbroken and a single father.

Anant and Nandini had been his family, his support, during those tough times. Ashraf managed to survive, and moved on, immersing himself completely in his work. And of course, Naima, who was his reason to breathe. Although at times, he felt she deserved the love of both parents. But that, he guessed, was what life was. *Unfair.*

'Who's hungry?' Ashraf laughed as he lifted his daughter and sat her down on his bike, in front of him. 'Meee!' she screamed, clapping her tiny hands. For the next two hours, Ashraf saw the world through his little girl's eyes; he saw innocence and excitement, and forgot all about the dangerous, uncertain world he lived in.

'Come home soon, Abbu,' Naima kissed him on the cheek when he dropped her home. He planted a kiss on her forehead, smiled and gave her a mock salute. 'Yes, boss!'

He left for the ATS headquarters, where a meeting had been called to finalise the security arrangements for the mega event. *The Mumbai marathon and inauguration of the much-awaited Mumbai Coastal Road.* While the city was excitedly looking forward to the event in three days' time, the cops were on tenterhooks, preparing for the worst and praying it would not come to that.

44

The conference room at the ATS headquarters was cramped for space. Key members of the ATS, the Mumbai police force, the CRPF and the Special Protection Group (SPG) had gathered in the room, filling it to the rafters. The SPG was involved as the prime minister would make a visit to the state's capital for the inauguration of the Mumbai Coastal Road. The special force, formed to provide proximate security to the prime minister, was under the direct supervision of the central government. The director of the SPG had joined the meeting via video conference. The home minister, Namit Jha, was also expected to join over a video line.

Jha had involved himself personally to oversee the security arrangements in light of the increased concerns due to the recent events, and the high threat level assessed by the SPG and the Intelligence Bureau. Given the involvement of multiple forces, Jha had designated Sarathi to lead the coordination efforts of the various units.

The meeting commenced the moment Jha joined in. Sarathi detailed the security arrangements planned for the event. Jha listened intently, asking questions and making notes from time to time. The Mumbai police commissioner also debriefed Jha on the arrangements for the general public as well as the marathon participants.

Sarathi invited Anant to fill everyone in on the final troop deployment strategy. Anant was in the middle of outlining the details of the strategy when he felt the phone in his back pocket vibrate; he ignored it. Even with the cell phone on silent mode, it distracted him. As the phone continued to buzz, he reached into his pocket and switched it off. He continued with his update for the next fifteen minutes. Everyone in the room consented with the plan; it was the best they could do. Sitting next to Anant, Dalvi creased his brows as he listened in on the discussions.

'Thank you for the update. If there is anything else that I can help with, let me know. All the best,' Jha said as he concluded the meeting and disappeared from the screen. Anant gathered his papers and walked out with Sarathi and the police commissioner, both of whom went to Sarathi's office.

It was only after Anant sat down at the desk in his office that he switched on his phone. And then he saw the message.

45

The Worli dairy, inaugurated in 1960, grew to become one of the major processing centres for dairy products in the country. At one time, there were three dairies in Mumbai, with huge amounts of milk processed at the Worli facility alone. With hundreds of workers, production at the plant ran into three shifts. But with the entry of private players, the state-run enterprises faced steep competition, and their losses started to mount. Now, the dairy at Kurla had shut down, and the Worli plant was functioning only partially – one daily shift from 4 p.m. to midnight.

The fourteen-acre land block in a prime location was worth a fortune, and the state government had made at least three attempts to sell the land to revive the state-owned milk brand or fund the Mumbai metro project. Plans to build a convention centre on the land had also been floated around. But none of these came through. Recently, the Adhikari-led government had announced plans to develop the plot as an international tourist complex.

While new ideas were discussed and plans formulated and discarded, the years had been unkind to the dairy. Most of the buildings in the facility were abandoned, and the structures lay in wait for a reason to stay standing. Only a section of the four-storeyed main building was functional – a part of the processing plant on the ground level, and an admin office and the packaging unit on the first floor. A wide peripheral roadway – that looked more like a desolate terrace now – ran around the structure on the first level. This open space provided easy access at multiple points from the packing unit to the refrigerated vehicles. The vehicles, a mix of trucks and tempos, transported the milk packets to various retail outlets and distribution centres, with scheduled pickups from the dairy between the shift hours.

Directly behind the dairy was an elevated public park, where M had been waiting for the past few hours, observing the production of the day being loaded into the vehicles. The delayed rains had finally hit the city that evening, and there was a light drizzle since evening. It was after 1:30 a.m. when the last of the delivery trucks left that Friday morning, the 28 of June. M waited for some more time, allowing the last of the workers to depart, after which she made her way towards the complex. She walked down the slight slope, careful to avoid the newly formed puddles, and climbed the wall into the dairy compound.

The only security cabin in the complex was on the other side, at the main entrance. M entered the old building, and felt she was stepping into a whole other world. The building was empty, but for a few operational pieces of factory equipment. The moonlight was sufficient to guide M until she reached the stairway. Once there, she switched on her penlight. Somewhere above, a tube light flickered. She climbed the three storeys to the top floor where the door at the landing was blocked by stacks of files and broken furniture. A thick layer of dust had settled on them. She heaved them aside, and pushed the door, its rusted hinges creaking as it opened. She went inside, slow and silent. The air inside was different; it smelled like a combination of metal and milk.

She closed the door behind her. Rain dripped down through cracks in the ceiling, and the tiled floor was wet in places. M walked along the row of glass windows, most of them cracked or shattered. She stopped at one of them and stared out. Around two hundred metres ahead, the main street, illuminated in yellow, stretched across the width of her vision. From the height, she could see over the barricades, where the street forked into the

Mumbai Coastal Road. She smiled when she saw the outline of the junction, where, in a little over forty-eight hours, the Mumbai marathon would be flagged off by the prime minister of India.

46

'It's not looking good, Mr Kulkarni,' the doctor said, gently patting Anant on the shoulder. Anant sank down, clutching the cold arm of the hospital chair for support. *Was this it?* He couldn't bring himself to answer that question. He had suppressed the thought of losing Nandini whenever it cropped up. He knew she would somehow make it through; she was a fighter. But the process of watching your loved one waste away, slowly dying right in front of your eyes, was cruel, and not something that Anant was prepared to handle.

He managed to stand up, and thanked his friend and neighbour who had responded to their house-help's call when Nandini's condition had worsened. *'Taking Nandini to Tata. Come there directly'* – was the urgent message he had received from the neighbour, and Anant had rushed to the Tata Memorial Hospital from the ATS headquarters.

Steeling himself, he entered the room. He watched the woman he loved so desperately lying asleep on the bed. A nurse sat beside her, looking tired, but she still smiled at Anant. Inspite of the morphine, Nandini appeared deep in agony; her breath coming in ragged, shallow gasps. Anant stood next to her, and caressed her forehead. The nurse offered him the only chair in the room, which Anant gratefully accepted. He sat by Nandini's side, quietly holding her hand.

Seconds passed until she opened her eyes and smiled at him. Anant nodded, but he couldn't speak. It was all he could do to hold back his tears.

'All set for the big day?' she asked softly.

'Let's see what happens,' Anant shrugged. She was always very interested in his work, and was keenly following his progress on the arrangements for the mega event in Mumbai in two days' time.

'I will watch it *live*,' she said, glancing towards the television in the room.

'We both will.'

Nandini shook her head. 'You have to be where you should be,' she said, 'hopefully, this time around I will see you also on TV.'

Anant thought his heart would explode at how she was making light of the situation. And he knew there was nothing he could do to make her relent. She was telling him to accept life and move on. No more walks in the park, no more anniversary celebrations, no more filter coffees together. Fifteen years of love, and he wondered if he would leave the hospital room alone.

47

Nostalgia washed over Navtej Singh as he eased the monster truck into the parking lot of the batch plant one last time. Every morning for the last four years, he had driven the mixer truck from the plant to the Mumbai Coastal Road construction site. The routine had remained the same. Every day, the cement, water and the aggregate would be loaded into the rotating barrel mounted on the truck chassis. The blades inside the barrel mixed the materials as the truck travelled to the jobsite. Once at the site, the concrete was poured from the truck through chutes, with the blades reversed to help push the concrete out of the barrel. The barrel kept the concrete liquid and ready to pour when it reached the site. After the day's job was done, Navtej drove the truck back to the batch plant for a refill. At times, he had done multiple trips during the day; and then there were nights when he slept in the truck at the plant. Tonight was different though; there was no refill to be done anymore.

He had seen the engineering marvel take shape foot-by-foot, and was proud of the role he had played in its creation, along with thousands of other labourers and engineers. And their collective efforts were going to be celebrated in a few hours with the inauguration of the Coastal Road. Navtej looked forward to the event.

He jumped down from the truck, and looked at it fondly. He ran his hands over the white – rusted and dented at places – bodywork, and decided to tell the contractor to send it to the reconditioning yard. *You have led a hero's life, my friend,* he whispered to his faithful companion.

Navtej turned around as he heard footsteps approaching him. He was surprised to see a man in running gear coming towards him. Wearing a half-sleeved t-shirt, shorts and sneakers, he waved out to Navtej, pointing to his mobile phone. The man had a sheet of paper with a number tagged to his t-shirt. Navtej had seen such tags on runners. *He must be running the Mumbai race,* Navtej guessed. *But what is he doing so far away from the starting point at this hour?*

'*Paaji*, can you help me?' the man said, showing the screen of his phone to Navtej.

Navtej smiled and walked towards the advancing man.

'Can you guide me to this address?' the man asked, and handed over his phone to the friendly driver.

As Navtej took the phone in his hand, Bandhu thrust a knife into his stomach. As the tip of the blade sank deep, Navtej screamed, but there was nobody there to hear his screams. Bandhu twisted the blade in his hands, all the while sinking it deeper and deeper into the helpless man's torso. Then, without warning, he jerked it all the way in, until the shiny metal had disappeared inside him and the grey handle pushed against his broken skin. Navtej's cry was a combination of guttural chokes mixed with an agonized roar.

Bandhu smirked, and pulled the blade out. Navtej sank to his knees, no longer screaming, with thick blood flowing freely from the gaping hole in his body. Bandhu jumped back as scarlet liquid gushed out in all directions, some of which squirted on his arms.

Bandhu waited for a few minutes, until the convulsing and trembling man was finally still. He dragged the dead man by the shoulders, and positioned the body by the foot-rest at the rear of the truck. Navtej Singh, with his lifeblood leaking out of him, sat still with his back resting against his beloved truck. Worried that his clothes would be bloodied, Bandhu took off his t-shirt, careful not to tear the running BIB. Bandhu climbed the two feet up on the chassis, and grunted as he hauled his victim up. He then moved to the other side, and with a screaming effort, he grabbed the body by the armpits, and lifted it up to its standing position. He caught his breath for a few seconds, facing the dead man staring down at him. And then, he lifted the body a foot off the ground and shoved it, head first, into the barrel of the mixer truck.

Bandhu found a half-filled bottle of water on the front seat, and washed the blood off his arms and chest, before putting on his t-shirt again. Humming his favourite song, he sat down at the driver's seat and switched on the overhead panel lights. He turned on the switch for charging the barrel, and in an instant, the spiral blade for mixing concrete started to spin. As the barrel rotated, the body of Navtej Singh was pushed deeper into the drum, the blades simultaneously chopping and grinding it.

***

Bandhu took out his burner phone and sent a missed call to a number. *M's number.* He had been warned to use the phone only once, for the purpose it had just served. *The second leg of M's plan was now set in motion.*

The truck made its way out of the parking lot onto the western express highway. The clock on the dashboard showed it was 2 a.m. Bandhu ran a quick estimate in his head; the race would be flagged off at 5:30 a.m. After thirty minutes, by 6 a.m., all the marathoners would be on the Coastal Road, crossing the mid-way to Versova, the halfway mark. More than thirty thousand runners would be on an isolated stretch. *That's when I will start,* Bandhu nodded to himself.

He was bowled over by the simplicity of M's plan. *Or rather, the other person's – the mastermind – who he knew existed and was pulling the strings, but with whom he had never interacted.* No guns. No bombs. No weapons – none at all! Just this monster truck, and thousands of hapless citizens. Runners. Caught on a bridge with nowhere to escape from a speeding truck, that would mow them down without mercy. The only way out for them was to jump off the sides of the elevated Coastal Road into the sea. *And he was sure not many would survive that.* In the worst case – he laughed at how he thought of *'worst case'* – he estimated a kill-rate of more than a few thousands. *Hell, he was sure he would surpass the 3000 killed in the 9/11 attacks. With just one truck.*

And the icing on the cake was that he had an escape plan. He was not going to get caught. He was sure he could pull it off. That's where the registration for the marathon and the running gear, with the BIB, would play a crucial part. There were no cameras along most of the stretch of the new road. At an opportune moment, after he had accomplished his mission, Bandhu intended to jump down from the moving truck, and be one amongst the panic-stricken runners. He would blend right in with the ill-fated crowd, screaming and running for his life.

48

The few hours leading up to the biggest event the city had ever seen brought in a range of emotions for Mumbaikars. Many of them planned to be at Worli for the inauguration of the Mumbai Coastal Road, a dream that was finally a reality. The remaining wanted to catch the event 'live' on television.

Alarms were set for as early as 2 a.m. By 4 a.m., the local trains, special buses organized for the event and the roads would be as busy as on a regular working day; and by 5 a.m., throngs of participants would have assembled at the starting point for the marathon. With the organisers learning from past experience, the starting point was now divided into various zones, based on the category of the race and the expected time entered by the participant to finish the run, with the faster ones being allowed to start sooner.

More than sixty thousand runners and marathoners, including half of them doing just the fun Dream Run of 6 kms, tried to retire early, to catch up on some sleep before the race. Not many got the shut-eye they needed though, in anticipation of the big day, where unbeknown to them, a monster truck waited.

***

Ranga did not sleep at all. His vision was to take shape in a few hours, and he wanted it to be executed flawlessly. His phone was constantly buzzing with updates he had asked for, and when an update was delayed even by a few minutes, he would dial the team himself. *Stage setup. Flag-off ceremony. Invitees' confirmation. Transport arrangements. Security for the VIPs. Facilities for the participants. Hydration stations. Medical facilities. Prize distribution. Media coverage. Philanthropy partners.* Ranga was on top of every single thing. The Sethna Mumbai Marathon would be the top sporting event in the world. He would not settle for anything less.

Most importantly, he was in continuous dialogue with Adhikari, and the PMO. He wanted to make sure everything went smoothly on those fronts. After the killings of Raut and Pawar, and the heightened threat levels for the event, he had momentarily rued his decision to combine the Mumbai Marathon with the inauguration of the Coastal Road. But the response from the people of Mumbai had not dampened, and tight security arrangements were in place. He was looking forward to a relaxed evening, sipping a quiet drink once the SMM was over.

***

Adhikari had dinner with Manjiri and Aashi; the trio laughing and chatting for a long time. Afterwards, he insisted that the three of them watch a movie together. He made a spirited pitch to play his favourite – a thriller – but it was his teenaged daughter who had the final say. As Adhikari navigated the OTT and hit the play button on the rom-com, Manjiri brought out a bowl of popcorn, which the family promptly dug into. Adhikari sat with his arms around the two ladies, and as he looked at them, he wished he could freeze time.

He tried his best not to cause any alarm at home, but he couldn't shake off the feeling that something was going to happen. And that he would be at the centre of it.

***

Prime minister Mahendra Doshi reclined on his seat, and looked out at the dark skies. He couldn't sleep, not just that night, but for the past few weeks; ever since he suspected there was a traitor in his midst. He was angry, of course; but more than that, he was saddened. *A party he had built over decades, how did it come to this?*

'We will be landing shortly at Mumbai,' the pilot announced.

'Can I get you something, sir? A coffee, perhaps?' the air-hostess smiled at Doshi.

'No, thank you... I am fine,' Doshi smiled back. *Some more time would be nice,* he thought.

***

'Ashraf, you, along with your team, will stand guard at the Versova junction of the Coastal Road,' Anant re-iterated as part of his final briefing to the forces on the night of Saturday, 29 June.

'Yes, sir,' Ashraf nodded. Initially, he was not too happy about being at the other end, when all the 'action' was expected to take place at Worli. But after a brief discussion with Anant, when he had first announced the positions a day earlier, he had seen merit in the decision. *I want all bases covered,* Anant had told him.

'How is apa?' Ashraf asked Anant, after everyone had left.

'Not very good,' Anant shook his head sadly.

'Shouldn't you be with her?'

'I want to... but you know your apa... she won't listen.'

'Yeah...,' Ashraf nodded knowingly and smiled slightly. 'Is there anything I can do?'

'Pray for her.'

'I will... I always do,' Ashraf said, and left for home.

He had been up, without any respite, for the last two nights, and desperately needed a short nap at the very least. It was close to 11 p.m. when he reached home. Keeping the door to his room open, he walked over to his neighbour's to pick up Naima. She was asleep. Not wanting to wake her up, he wrapped her in a blanket and carried the sleeping child home. She stirred slightly as he put her on the single bed. He kissed her forehead, and tucked her in. He had to be at Versova by 4 a.m.; he set the alarm for an hour before and spread out the mattress on the floor, where he usually slept. He dozed off as soon as his head hit the pillow.

***

In Beijing, Chen Jintao was in a buoyant mood. He had cleared his diary for the first half; he intended to follow the news from India 'live' on television, and wanted to hear it first-hand when the mission was accomplished. He had, in fact, gone one step further. He had fixed an appointment with President Xi that afternoon. He wanted to break the news, in person, to the President, and of course, exaggerating his own role in the meticulous planning and flawless execution. The Indian roadblock to the BRI – President Xi's vision for global domination – would be cleared. And it was all thanks to him. Chen Jintao. *He could not wait for the meeting.*

***

After leaving the plant, Bandhu drove the truck for another fifteen minutes, at a steady speed, along the desolate western express highway. The city had seen intermittent showers in the last two days, and the downpour was heavier that night. He turned right on a flyover, and passing over the railway lines below, crossed over to the western side of the suburb. He kept going until he reached the waterfront, where he turned left again.

He slowed down when he saw the bright yellow spot appearing on the windscreen. *The Versova end of the Mumbai Coastal Road.* Bandhu switched off the headlights, and pulled over to the side of the road. While he waited, he set the volume of the radio above the noise of the falling rain.

***

M screwed open the thermos and sipped the black coffee, gone cold a day earlier. She bit into the last piece of the boiled chicken she had carried with her, crumpled the wrapping foil and put it back into the side-pocket of her backpack. She focused her binoculars on the main street, awash in bright yellow. She had witnessed the frenetic activity along the street in the last twenty-four hours. Traffic from both ends had been cordoned off, and the only vehicles allowed were those pre-registered to supply equipment and material for the mega event, VIP cars and of course, police vans. Since the night before the event, pedestrian entry along the street was restricted to only residents. Anticipating this level of tightened security measures closer to the event, M had chosen to be 'on location' *two days prior*. It was a part of the plan.

She knelt down, and looked through the telescopic lens of her sniper rifle. She adjusted her tripod one last time to tip her vision over the treetop in the complex, onwards to the elaborate stage that was set up for the inauguration. The rain was coming down harder, and while it was something M had considered and accounted for, she hoped it would stop in time. The open terrace above the floor where she was, in fact, provided the best view of her target. But it also increased the chances of being spotted by someone in the neighbouring building, although it was some distance away. In her professional opinion, she had chosen the optimal location, carefully balancing the risk and the reward. Her thoughts, for a moment, drifted to what she intended to do with the reward, and she smiled. An event organiser on the stage, unaware that her heart was in the crosshairs of M's rifle vision, shared a laugh with a colleague.

***

'I will... I always do,' Ashraf said, and left. Anant went through his messages and call log once again; there was nothing from the hospital. He followed Ashraf out of the ATS headquarters, and headed straight for the hospital. He was pleasantly surprised to see Nandini awake. Lying down on her bed, she was watching videos of Hindi movie songs on the television.

'What are you doing up so late?' Anant asked, smiling at his wife.

'Not sleepy... and it's only eleven, Mr Kulkarni,' Nandini said cheekily.

'Have you eaten? Are you feeling good?'

'Yes... to both... now stop your interrogation and tell me if *you* have eaten something?'

'Not yet.'

'Let me call for some dinner for you,' Nandini said, looking at the intercom on her side-table, and holding the cold metal rod of her bed, she tried to sit up.

'It's a hospital, not a hotel,' Anant joked, and placed two pillows behind Nandini as she sat up.

'Is it not? Could have fooled me,' Nandini playfully rolled her brown eyes in shocked surprise, and laughed.

Anant looked at her, and smiled. It wasn't just the sound of her laughter; it was her expression, the way her eyes filled with joy, and the unshed tear on the verge of spilling down her left cheek. It was as if the frail woman had reserved her strength all day to smile with him. 'I will be back in a minute,' he told her and left the room. He returned with a sandwich and a bottle of water. Nandini shook her head when he offered her a bite, but took a nibble when Anant insisted. He went on to tell her about their preparedness to combat the threat, which, as always, she listened to intently.

'You should get home and rest for a few hours before the big day starts,' Nandini told Anant.

'I have a better idea,' Anant said, and helped her lie down. He then sat down on the chair next to her bed, spread his legs, and winked at her. She reached out for his arm with a shaking hand, and held it until both of them fell asleep.

***

The Serpent was unable to sleep that night. He paced around his room, waiting impatiently for dawn. He could almost read the headlines that would dominate world news in a few hours. *India's leading prime ministerial candidate assassinated. Prime Minister Doshi likely to continue as the country's leader if the IPP emerges victorious at the polls.* And the Serpent knew that Doshi was not in a position to continue as the prime minister. *Prime minister Doshi was dying. His days were numbered. A few months at best,* the Serpent knew.

And that was the beauty of the Serpent's master-stroke. He did not see any point in getting Doshi killed; once the news of his terminal illness was out, he would not be chosen as the prime minister – neither by the Indian public, nor by his own party. But Adhikari, when elected, which was only a matter of time, would have a long run as the country's leader. And Adhikari, like Doshi, would not sign off on China's BRI ambitions. But get Adhikari out of the way, and there was nobody else to thwart his ambition to the top job. And Khorgos would be his after the BRI was signed off. *Signed off by none other than the Serpent – India's new prime minister.*

49

A nant woke up with a start as his phone vibrated; it was his morning alarm. He had kept it on vibrate-only as he did not want to wake up Nandini. In the dim lights, he looked at his sleeping wife and realized how vulnerable she had become, and how much of a toll the sickness had taken. He freshened up, tucked in his shirt and wore his shoes. He stroked Nandini's forehead and left the room, closing the door gently behind him.

As he drove towards Worli, he called all his unit leaders to check on the arrangements. He heaved a sigh of relief when everyone confirmed their readiness. He made a quick call to Sarathi and gave him an update of the situation. The prime minister was due to land in Mumbai at 5 a.m., by which time Adhikari would already be at the venue. Calls made, updates given and taken, it was 4 a.m. when Anant got down from the police car, around five hundred metres from the Coastal Road junction. He walked the remaining distance, visually inspecting the area and the security detail, as the cops at the first barricade saluted him. He stopped and gave instructions at every checkpoint as he moved forward. He passed the Coastal Road junction and followed the same procedure for half a kilometre on the other side.

As the clock ticked, a sea of runners started to converge around the starting point near the junction, and Anant realized pretty quickly why the Mumbai marathon was the largest mass sporting event in Asia. A huge banner near the stage announced – *The Greatest Race on Earth*. All the runners had to undergo a security clearance before they entered the starting zones, which were set up in a vacant plot adjacent to the Worli dairy complex. A dual security check was set up at the entry gates. First, the participants had to pass through the walk-through metal detectors that were set up at the entry gates to the zones. Next, a few metres in, there was a bag deposit-cum-collection counter, for runners carrying their bags. All bags were checked manually, and there were trained sniffer dogs with their handlers doing the rounds in the area. Random checks were also conducted by a team of security officials, who were armed with hand-held metal detectors. Participants were specifically notified to report earlier than usual due to the enhanced security measures. As Anant passed through the entrance, surveying the arrangements, he could hear a few runners grumbling about the long queues that had now begun to form at the entry points.

Anant was satisfied with the checks at the entrance. He thought of the other precautions he had taken as he started to walk back towards the junction, where the race flag-off was to happen, in front of the main stage. Spectators wanting to witness the event had to undergo a similar personal scrutiny when they entered the main street from either end. No vehicles had been allowed to be parked on the main street since the previous evening. The Coastal Road ran with the Arabian sea along its edge on the other side, and an attack from that end was unlikely. However, Anant had stationed two patrol boats to do rounds along the stretch, just in case.

Anant saw that Ranga had arrived and was having a spirited discussion with a fellow business magnate and the latest Bollywood sensation, who was also the face of the Sethna Mumbai Marathon. A large crowd, a mix of runners and spectators, had gathered around the trio and were taking pictures and selfies. As soon as Ranga saw Anant, he waved to him and excusing himself, walked towards him.

'All set?' Ranga asked. He had to almost shout to make himself heard above the Bollywood chartbusters that were being played at full volume at the venue.

'Yes, so far so good,' Anant gave him a thumbs up sign. Just then, they could hear the police siren wailing, and a cavalcade of three cars stopped on the opposite side of the road. Dalvi jumped out of the middle car, and opened the door for Adhikari. As the chief minister stepped out, the public greeted him with a loud cheer. He waved out enthusiastically to the crowd, smiling broadly. Two security guards, armed with machine guns, walked beside him. Adhikari saw Ranga and Anant, and walked towards them. He shook Anant's hand, and gave Ranga a warm hug.

'Congratulations, my friend. Your dream has finally come true,' Adhikari patted Ranga on the arm.

'So has yours, Mr Chief Minister... or rather, *Mr Prime Minister*,' Ranga laughed.

The two friends were joined by a few other celebrities. Anant excused himself and was about to leave when Dalvi came over to Adhikari and said, 'The prime minister has landed, and is on his way. He should be here in less than fifteen minutes.'

'Let the show begin,' Adhikari said. Ranga beamed. Anant thought about the assassin still on the loose. *Where was she now?*

50

The heavy rain in the night had given way to a light drizzle; the temperature had dropped and the air was cooler, much to the delight of the runners. The participants were warming up for the start, most of them doing stretching exercises. The fastest category of runners, including those from across the world, known as the Elite Runners, had assembled at the starting line. They would be the first off the block, with access to an empty stretch ahead of them in their quest for winning the race.

The contestants let out a cheerful shout as the announcer, a famous radio jockey, invited the movie star on stage. As the DJ played one of his chartbusters, he broke into an impromptu jig, much to the delight of the crowd. Ranga and Adhikari, surrounded by their security detail, were waiting for Doshi, before they went on stage. Anant and Sarathi were in discussion with the unit heads of the CRPF and the SPG. A detection dog handler, after a satisfactory check of the stage and the area around it, gave an all-clear signal to the SPG head.

Anant looked at his watch, it was almost 5:45 a.m. and the flag-off was already delayed. Nobody seemed to mind it, though. The only remaining vantage point that Anant wanted to inspect that morning was a newly constructed high-rise. The building was at the Coastal Road junction, on the opposite side of the main street from where the stage was. The street took a sharp turn where the building ended, so the apartments further down did not offer a direct line of sight to the dais, and did not pose any security threat. Anant crossed the road with a team of two ATS officers.

'Check out every flat with a balcony or window facing the sea, and confirm there has been no intrusion. Give me an affirmation once it's done,' he instructed. The two officers nodded and sprinted in through the building entrance.

Next to the building, directly opposite the stage, was the Worli dairy. Anant's team had surveyed the abandoned complex two weeks ago, and had reported it as a 'safe zone'. Trees lined most of the façade, blocking the view of a marksman on the open terrace of the building. Besides, anyone on the terrace ran a huge risk of being spotted. Anant decided to have a word with the personnel in the security cabin nevertheless. The two men were standing outside the cabin, in front of the closed iron gates. They confirmed they had not seen anything suspicious, and they had been awake the whole night. Satisfied with their answer, Anant asked them to be alert and report to the cops immediately in case they found anything irregular.

As the day broke that cloudy morning, the once blue building of the Worli dairy became more than just a dark outline, with dark patches of grey in its background. From the ground, Anant squinted at the top floor of the derelict structure with a row of shattered windows running across its length. Directly in front of the windows, around fifty metres ahead, the frontage was lined with old trees that were as tall, clearly obstructing the line of sight of anyone in the building. *The building does offer an opportunity to hide,* Anant acceded. *And for a sharpshooter on the uppermost floor... would it be possible to get a clean shot?*

Not wanting to leave anything to chance, Anant decided to follow through on his instinct. As the security guard opened the iron gate for him, all pandemonium broke loose outside. Prime minister Doshi had just arrived to a rousing welcome. Without breaking his pace, Anant turned around to see the prime minister waving out to the crowd.

Anant had visited the dairy in its prime, when he was in school. The entrance which was once something to be marvelled at, presented a sorry sight, with the marble steps chipped away and paint peeling off. He could almost cut through the thick layer of suffocating dust as he climbed up the staircase. He could hear his footsteps echoing as he raced up till the landing below the top floor, after which he slowed down, and made his way up in silence. He saw the files and pieces of furniture carelessly strewn aside, clearing the way to the only door on the floor. He drew out his service revolver and held it with both hands, in front of him. Anant tip-toed to the door, and using his right shoulder, pushed it open.

51

After an hour of crouching on her knees in the dark, M felt thirsty. Holding the rifle with her right hand, pressed against her shoulder, she reached out for the bottle of water with her left, and took a deep swig. Her wait was finally over, when she saw the prime minister's convoy arriving. She heard the rapturous welcome he received, and wondered if the man she was about to kill would ever match up to Doshi's level of popularity.

The rain had subsided considerably in the last few hours, and with daybreak, she no longer needed the night vision clip-on sniper scope. *Both factors favourable,* she smiled. But while the visibility had improved outside, the only light source for the dank, dark building were the cracks within the ceiling and the fragmented window panes allowing jagged rays of light into the building. M, with her breathing steady, and mind focused, lay completely still. Through the lens of her rifle, she saw the prime minister, followed by the chief minister and the chairman of the Sethna group climb on to the stage. The prime minister took centre-stage, and in his trademark style, kept waving to the crowd, until the cheering subsided. After a short speech, he stepped aside, and as per the itinerary, invited Adhikari to initiate the proceedings, leading up to the inauguration of the Coastal Road and flag-off of the Mumbai Marathon. Ranga stood next to Doshi, beaming with pride.

As Adhikari came forward, he stepped right into the centre of the circular lens of M's sniper rifle. M targeted the chief minister's heart in the crosshairs. *She had him, but she would not squeeze the trigger yet. The race had to commence before she pulled the trigger. Killing Adhikari now would mean the event would be called off, and Bandhu's leg of the plan would fail. The marathoners had to be at a*

197

point of no return on the Coastal Road, running, with the speeding truck hurtling towards them, when she had to get Adhikari. It was difficult – the wait. But that was the plan. And she would stick to it.

In complete silence, M's rifle followed Adhikari as he shifted. The calm was shattered by the creaking of the door. M turned to see a new figure, leaning against the door, tall and muscular, a male without a doubt.

***

Anant pressed forward through the door into the murky hall, gun drawn, expecting to find nobody. He was momentarily surprised when he saw the silhouetted figure in the gloom, crouching and unmoving. Senses sharpened with adrenaline, he ducked in the shadows, careful not to make another sound. But he realized it was too late, as the figure ahead stood up and raised in his direction, what was unmistakably a rifle. *It was definitely the woman. The killer.*

***

With early daylight streaking in through the shattered window panes, M's shadowy figure emerged against a very contrasting background. Meanwhile, she had just removed the night vision clip-on from her rifle. She had to adjust her vision to the darkness inside the hall, as she tried to trace the man. This difference of a split second was enough for a professional. She cursed out loud as the last thing she saw was a yellow-red light that spat out in the darkness, and tore through her forehead.

52

'And now, I invite our beloved and honourable prime minister, Shri Mahendra Doshi ji, to say a few words,' Adhikari welcomed the prime minister as he completed his address. As Doshi stood up, he saw Sarathi walking towards him, Anant by his side. Sarathi gestured to the prime minister, requesting a moment to speak. Doshi nodded and called them forward; he also asked Adhikari to join them.

'Sir, we have some good news... we got her,' Sarathi said, as the foursome huddled together on the stage.

'That's excellent news... well done,' Doshi exclaimed.

'All thanks to Anant here,' Sarathi said, patting Anant on the back.

'Superb news... and a big relief,' Adhikari said, shaking Anant's hands. Doshi, too, smiled and acknowledged Anant's efforts.

'Who all know that the threat is averted?' Doshi asked, looking at Sarathi and Anant.

'Just the four of us, as of yet,' Anant answered.

'Let's keep it that way for the time being. We don't want a panic situation if news of the assassination attempt leaks out.'

'Sir, from our raid at the Wadala residence where they were hiding, we know that the assassin was working with two more accomplices. One of them, Tamas, has been killed. But there is one more man... it is important we get him as well... in my opinion, sir, we should cancel the event... it's a huge risk to continue,' Anant said.

'Risk? What is the risk now? She is dead... she was the one who killed both Raut and Pawar... one of her accomplices is dead... the second one may just be a helper, after all, who has played his part... look at the public... they are so charged up,'

Adhikari said, 'and if we cancel now citing the real reason, there will be pandemonium anyway. Also, what other reason can we give to call it off now? Either way, there will be a severe backlash on the polls if we don't go ahead.'

'You have done a great job, Anant,' Doshi said after reflecting on the situation for a few moments, 'but now that the danger has passed, we should continue as planned.'

Adhikari and Sarathi nodded their agreement; Anant did not look too convinced. A few feet away, Ranga was shuffling impatiently, looking at the quartet with a puzzled expression on his face. 'Ranga,' Doshi called out to him, 'let's get the race started, and Sanjay, let's show the world Mumbai's Coastal Road.'

***

The Serpent leaned forward and increased the television's volume as he saw the "Breaking News" banner flash on the screen. *The city wakes up to a breath-taking new morning. Mumbai marathoners have the first glimpse of the Coastal Road.* The channel then showed snippets of the prime minister's speech, and the inauguration of the Coastal Road. The camera zoomed in on the race's starting line, as the runners first set foot on the city's dream project. The Serpent switched off the television as an interviewer asked Adhikari the opening question.

It was a matter of around an hour, for his plan to be executed. In that time, M would have pulled the trigger, and Adhikari would be dead. At the same time, his dual strike would play an all-important role; because if the unthinkable happened – if M failed – Bandhu's truck attack would then become his primary weapon. He did feel slight pangs of regret when he had initially planned the massacre of so many civilians, but it was another sure-fire way to ensure Adhikari did not get the prime ministership. Not with so many innocent lives lost under his watch, on *his* new road. *No way.*

He began to relax. *It will all work out,* he reassured himself. He looked at his watch; there was still time. The Serpent helped himself to a hearty breakfast as he waited for news of Adhikari's assassination, and the Mumbai Marathon carnage.

53

Anant went through the contents of M's backpack, but did not find any clue to her identity, or who she was working for. The only thing of any use was the cheap handphone he found on her; although he knew it would be a burner, paid for in cash with no record connecting it to M. He was not pinning too many hopes on it leading anywhere. He had dismantled the rifle from the tripod stand and had arranged every item neatly in a row, next to M's lifeless body.

He looked at his phone; there was no message or call from the hospital. He wanted to wind up the proceedings here, hand over his charge to someone else and head back to be by Nandini's side as soon as possible. He had made up his mind to take time off to be with her, until she recovered. It hurt him to even think about the alternative.

He paused just for a moment and looked out the window. It was spectacular – the engineering marvel that was the Coastal Road. It had been more than thirty minutes since the race was flagged off, and the last of the runners had long departed from sight. He was upset with Doshi's decision to continue with the race; his instincts told him it was not over yet. He prayed that he was wrong.

His thoughts were diverted to the vibration of a phone. Impulsively, he looked at his phone, but the screen was blank. *It was M's phone.* He grabbed her phone from the floor. *I am starting now.* The notification on the screen read. Anant's heartbeat picked up as he felt his worst fears coming true. She did have a co-conspirator. He made a mental note of the sender's phone number, and took out his phone.

'Note down this number... and trace its location... right now!'

he screamed as soon as the call was picked up. He rushed to the security units, and ordered them to evacuate the prime minister, chief minister, Ranga and all other dignitaries. 'Clear the area,' he shouted.

'What happened, Anant?' Sarathi asked, perplexed.

'Sir, I will explain later... trust me on this one... it's not over yet,' Anant exclaimed, his breathing ragged, 'can we do anything to recall the participants?' he asked Ranga, just as he was being whisked away by his security guards.

'No, we can send a few cars from here... but there are thousands of them out there...,' Ranga shrugged away the guards and stopped to speak with Anant.

Just then, Anant's phone buzzed. 'Traced it,' the caller said, 'the location is near Versova... it is headed along the highway towards the Coastal Road end, as we speak... going by the speed, whoever has the phone is in a fast-moving vehicle.'

54

It was the first time that Ashraf had seen the Coastal Road at Versova; until then, it had been barricaded. He had parked the police car at the intersection of the two branches of the road; one providing an exit at Versova and the second one arched onwards towards Kandivali, the final leg of the Coastal Road project. Ashraf estimated he would see the first group of runners in less than ten minutes.

Only an hour ago, the darkness was absolute, and it was cold and damp. Now, the clouds were clearing, revealing soft blue stripes in the sky. Ashraf opened the door, and got down from the driver's seat of the police car. The two other officers with him, one next to him in the front and the second one in the backseat, remained seated in the car. Ashraf crossed the front of the silver grill to the other side, and keeping his hands on the parapet, stared at the placid ocean, now golden in the first rays of the sun. *It's going to be a beautiful day... I will take Naima to the beach in the evening,* he decided. His thoughts were interrupted by Anant's phone call, warning him to stay alert, and that reinforcements were on their way. He was still on the call with Anant, when he saw a white truck speeding towards the junction.

The truck was gaining ground by the second, its black tyres squealing on the grey, rain-washed tarmac. Ashraf ran towards the front door of the police car, hoping to start it and get it into the way of the monster. But there was not enough time; the truck was too close. He drew out his service revolver, and standing in the middle of the road, pointed it at the oncoming truck. 'Get out of there,' he hollered at his fellow officers, who didn't understand what had changed in the last few seconds.

A flag tied to a pole at the front of the truck fluttered violently in the wind. The truck was dangerously close now; Ashraf could see the grinning man at the wheel, and he knew he was not going to stop. He aimed, and started to fire. He missed the first two shots; one went over the top of the truck and one hit the front grate. The third bullet shattered the windscreen, cracking it but missing the driver. The mixer truck was almost on him as Ashraf continued to fire; his next two bullets caught the man in the arm and the shoulder, causing him to veer off sharply. Ashraf jumped out of the way as the truck skidded and rammed into the police car, trapping the two officers between the car and parapet as they were trying to get down. Their screams of agony filled the air briefly; replaced soon with grunts and groans, and then silence.

The truck had swerved sideways, almost blocking the entire road. Ashraf, knocked on to the asphalt, was disorientated, and could feel warm blood oozing from his upper lip into his mouth. He got up and walked towards the crash. The side of the police car, where the truck had crashed into, was a mangled mess. One of his fellow officers was lying face down on the roof of the car, the other one's torso was spread over the parapet; both their lower bodies were stuck between the metal of the car and the concrete of the wall. The truck, its headlights smashed, sat still on the street, its engine sputtering and smoke blasting out from the exhaust pipe.

Ashraf walked to the front door of the truck and opened it. There was complete stillness. He was surprised to see the driver in running gear, but it did not take him long to realize what his plan must have been. *Bastard.* At that moment, Ashraf felt hatred as never before. The sudden movement stunned him. The bloodied man at the wheel rained kicks onto Ashraf's face and head, knocking down the cop backwards.

Bandhu jumped down, grimacing; his t-shirt and BIB were scarlet, and blood was still oozing out of the two punctured marks on his right side. He sat down on Ashraf's chest, making it hard for him to breathe. With his left hand, Bandhu continued to punch Ashraf, intending to smash him into the ground. Ashraf, with a frenzied scream, gathered all his might and lifted his upper body up, throwing Bandhu off balance. Jerking his head back, Ashraf head-butted Bandhu, who fell backwards. Bandhu blocked Ashraf's blows by lying down in a fetal position, waiting to ride out the storm of his attack. With all his focus on the man's damaged shoulder, Ashraf did not look at the man's left hand, with which he plunged a knife into Ashraf's shin as his leg was going to attack him one more time. Ashraf cried out in pain, and raised his injured leg, bringing his knee closer to his chest. Seizing the opportunity, Bandhu got up and with one swift motion, pulled the knife out of Ashraf's leg.

The street swam in and out of focus as Ashraf tried to limp away from his assailant. A few feet ahead, he saw his revolver lying on the tarmac, and hobbled towards it. He was getting slower with each step, and he could feel the presence behind him getting closer. He knew there was no way he could reach the gun in time, and so, with everything he had, he lunged forward desperately. He was disoriented horizontally for a moment before he fell, cracking on the hard surface. The gun was still just out of reach, and as Ashraf tried to drag himself ahead, he felt an arm grab his wounded leg, pulling it backwards.

Digging his left palm onto the surface, Ashraf made a determined plunge for the gun with his right. He spat out blood as he landed on his chin, but felt his fingers touch the cold metal. He swung around on his back, gun in hand, when he saw the man raise his left hand. In a flash, he thrust the knife into Ashraf's chest. As the blade tore through his flesh, Ashraf fired.

Ashraf saw the man's face being blown apart, before blankness engulfed him. Then he remembered Naima. *He had to get home. They had to go to the beach. Suddenly, he was sleeping on the floor at home. His hand reached out for his daughter, sleeping by his side. She wasn't there. He tried a few more times before he finally gave up.*

55

'The target is not moving anymore... the location of the phone is stationary... at the Versova junction of the Coastal Road, sir,' the cybercrime specialist told Anant. That could mean one of two possibilities; Ashraf and team had managed to neutralize the threat, or the target had gotten rid of the phone. He tried calling Ashraf, but he was not picking up his phone. The secondary unit was a few minutes away, and Anant expected a confirmation soon.

'Anant, good news. The first set of runners have crossed the Versova junction... we just got the update on our tracking system,' Ranga said. The e-tag embedded in the running BIBs of marathoners made it possible to track their location during the race. It also served the purpose of ensuring runners followed the correct path, and did not take any shortcuts, by placing detectors at various milestones along the track.

'That's great,' Anant let out a sigh of relief. He was almost certain Ashraf had done the job, and wanted to get confirmation that the situation was under control. He tried calling him again. *No answer.*

Doshi and Adhikari had been briskly escorted away by their security detail as soon as the news of a potential second threat emerged. Adhikari insisted on staying on, but Doshi prevailed and made sure the chief minister was safely taken away. Doshi himself left for the airport under enhanced protection. Ranga had refused to leave the stage. 'It is my event,' he had asserted, 'besides, there is no threat to me, so I will make sure everything goes on as smoothly as possible under the given circumstances.'

Anant answered his phone at the first ring. It was the officer in charge of the secondary unit despatched to Versova. 'Sir, the attack has been foiled. The suspect was driving a truck...our team

207

intercepted it at the entry to the road. We have checked the truck for explosives – there are none. And the suspect, a man of around forty, has been neutralised.'

'Congratulations to the team,' Anant said, pumping his fist in the air.

'But sir, I have some bad news as well...'

56

It was noon by the time Doshi's aircraft touched down in Delhi. He had been informed of the second attack that was thwarted, and felt incredibly fortunate that two deadly strikes had been averted that day. He shuddered to think about the enormous loss of lives had the truck attack not been foiled. *Thousands of innocent citizens.* He bowed his head to the almighty in a moment of gratitude. And if Adhikari had been assassinated, the party would have been in shambles right before the general elections. He was certain the party management would have insisted on him continuing as the prime minister had Adhikari been out of the picture. And in all fairness, he would have had to tell his party, and the Indian populace at large, about his terminal illness. But he was comforted to know that it would not come to that, and he would be able to hand over the administration smoothly to a worthy and able successor.

Flanked by security, Doshi disembarked from the aircraft. A convoy of three bullet-proof cars was waiting on the runway; Doshi smiled and waved out to his regular driver, who was holding a door open for him. It was when the prime minister was getting into his car that he collapsed.

***

As Adhikari felicitated the winners of the Mumbai Marathon, Jintao screamed out loud and flung a paperweight at the television, that was streaming a live broadcast of the ceremony. He could not believe it; *both* the strikes – so meticulously planned – had failed. It took him a few minutes to gather himself. He took a sip of water from a glass on his desk, and reflected on the options available to him now. He was worried about his upcoming meeting with President Xi, and the story he would have to spin for the paramount leader. He decided to buy some more time for himself; he called Xi's office and requested to reschedule his appointment for the following day. *I am not feeling too well,* he had offered as a reason for the postponement – which was not too far from the truth. Deciding to head home early, he left office.

'To the Central Office, sir?' his chauffeur asked, looking at Jintao in the rear-view mirror.

Jintao was staring out of the window, brooding over his next course of action.

'Sir?'

'No, home...,' Jintao grunted. Just then, his phone buzzed. Jintao listened without saying a word for the next few minutes. 'Thank you for letting me know,' he hung up at the end of it. *That was useful information indeed.* He smiled as a plan was beginning to form in his mind.

'Turn back... take me to the Central Office... quick!' he said brusquely to his chauffeur, who promptly changed lanes, took the next U-turn and sped towards Zhongnanhai.

Zhongnanhai, a former imperial garden in the city of Beijing, was adjacent to the Forbidden City. It served as the central headquarters for the Chinese Communist Party, and also housed the office of President Xi, along with the rest of the Chinese leadership. The executive assistant to Xi was surprised to see Jintao, who had, just a while ago, requested to reschedule his meeting.

'A matter of national importance has come up. It is imperative that I get some time with the President,' Jintao explained to the assistant.

After five minutes, he was shown into President Xi Liu's lavish office.

***

It took Chen Jintao a little over thirty minutes to tell President Xi about the Serpent's plan, starting with their train journey from Khorgos to Yining. He emphasized how immaculate the Serpent's plan was, and the level of detailing that had been incorporated into it. *A double attack, with a guarantee of at least one succeeding. Assigning M to the task. Why target Adhikari and not Doshi? That one was a real winner.* Jintao ended with the surprising turn of events that day, and how, everything that could possibly go wrong had gone so. Throughout his narration, he chose his words very carefully and left out parts that could amplify his own role in the failed strikes.

'That's all,' Jintao concluded. A bead of sweat dripped down his face as he waited for reaction from his paramount leader. Xi Liu's cold eyes stared at his foreign minister, the expression on his face inscrutable. Jintao felt his clasped hands quivering as he kept looking at the floor uneasily, fearing an outburst.

'You said you had a plan that would ensure none of this would lead back to China?' Xi asked in an icy tone.

'Yes... yes, I do,' Jintao said eagerly. *There was an escape, after all.*

'Tell me about it.'

***

'How are you feeling now, sir?'

'Well doctor, you know I can't say *"as good as new"*,' Doshi smiled, lifting himself up slightly on the hospital bed. Dr Mehta shook his head, and gave a wry smile. He had been Doshi's personal physician ever since the prime minister had assumed office. Today, he had taken charge the moment Doshi was brought to the hospital from the airport, and had worked with the specialist medical team at the hospital to oversee all the tests administered to get the prime minister back in action.

'I hope this is...,' Doshi started, when Dr Mehta interjected,

'Don't worry, sir...barring a few, nobody knows you have been admitted. And of course, there's nothing in the media.'

Doshi heaved a sigh of relief. 'And when can I resume work?'

'Well, it was mostly fatigue, and I know you won't take my advice to rest. So, tomorrow is a good day.'

'*Mostly?*' Doshi chuckled, and then seeing his doctor's crestfallen face, he said, 'I know it can be any day now... but I cannot thank you enough for your tireless efforts, and most importantly, for keeping it to yourself.'

'Sir, there's something... I need to talk to you about,' Dr Mehta said hesitatingly.

'Please go ahead, Doctor...'

Just then, there was a buzzing sound by Doshi's bedside table. It was his phone. He recognized the number. He glanced at the clock on the spotlessly white wall; it was past 9 p.m. Surprised, he picked up the phone, gesturing politely to Dr Mehta to give him privacy. The doctor nodded and left the room, chatting briefly with the prime minister's security staff stationed outside.

Once Doshi was certain the door was shut, he answered the phone. 'President Liu, what a pleasant surprise! But it must be nearing midnight in Beijing – hope everything is alright?'

'Everything is fine. I heard you had taken unwell, and wanted to enquire about your well-being – that's all.'

Though momentarily taken aback, Doshi quickly recovered, 'I am absolutely hale and hearty... thank you for checking,' Doshi said, wondering what could be the real reason Liu had called.

'That's good to hear. And now that you are feeling alright, let me come straight to the point,' Xi said. 'China has always been India's ally, and wished it well. MSS has just passed me classified intelligence about the thwarted twin attacks in Mumbai today.'

There was silence at both ends as the two world leaders waited. Xi, allowing the bomb he had dropped to have its effect; and Doshi, processing how Xi knew about the foiled attacks in

Mumbai. Doshi decided there was no point denying the near-miss events; he regained his composure and said, 'I am listening.'

'I am sure by now you would have figured out that the execution of such an elaborate plot would require the involvement of an insider... or better put – a *traitor*!' Xi hissed, seemingly outraged.

Xi is right on the money there, Doshi thought. He continued, 'Go on, Mr President.'

'Mr Prime Minister, between friends, I am going to tell you who it is... am sure you will handle the matter appropriately,' Xi said matter-of-factly, and paused for a moment, before he gave the name to Doshi.

Doshi felt the phone slipping out of his hand.

***

The next morning, Doshi, pensive and troubled, was in his office unusually early even by his standards. He had not slept the whole night at the hospital, and was feeling exhausted, not much from the previous day's health scare or from the happenings of the past few months, but from the conversation he had with Xi Liu. While the news of his hospitalisation was kept strictly restricted to only a few, he had received many messages wishing him a speedy recovery.

Doshi had deliberately not taken any hurried action on the information Xi had given him. A habit that had stood him in good stead was not to react to a situation impulsively. And this was too grave a matter to not give it a few hours of intense consideration. Finally, he made up his mind and dialled three digits on the intercom. It was answered at the first ring, as he had expected it to.

'Could you please come to my office?' Doshi asked the person at the other end, and hung up without waiting for an answer.

It took Namit Jha less than fifteen minutes to be seated

opposite the Prime Minister of India.

***

'I am so relieved to see you in office; yesterday was quite worrying,' Jha said, sounding genuinely concerned.

'I am okay now... but am getting old... not sure how much time I have left,' Doshi said in a sombre tone.

'Please don't say such unpleasant things,' Jha said, immediately embarrassed by his uncharacteristically emotional words. He abruptly changed the topic, 'You asked to meet me? Anything the matter?'

Doshi let out a deep sigh, and beckoned Jha to the three-seater sofa in his office. The two friends sat down, Jha's wide gaze fixated on Doshi, still confused why he had been summoned.

'These events of the last few months...,' Doshi started, '...have been quite disturbing, to say the least. We did well to avert the tragedy at Mumbai yesterday, but I am sure you have figured it out that the sheer audacity of the heinous plan was not possible – even to conceive, let alone coming so close to its execution – without an insider's involvement. Perhaps, this person even masterminded the attacks.'

'I agree... the thought did come to my mind,' Jha nodded in agreement. Doshi went on to tell Jha about the call he had received from Xi when he was in hospital.

'And I suppose it was the 'insider' who told Xi that you were hospitalised,' Jha concluded.

'Yes, I would think so,' Doshi concurred.

'I would love to lay my hands on that bastard,' Jha gritted his teeth in anger, his fists clenched.

Doshi smiled and said, 'You know what... Xi actually gave me a name.'

'Of the traitor?' Jha looked up in amazement at Doshi.

'Yes,' Doshi closed his eyes and nodded, a slight smile playing on his lips.

'Whose name did he give you?'

'Yours.'

***

There were a few seconds of stunned silence before the prime minister's office erupted. Jha was storming across the room, hurling the choicest of expletives at Xi Liu and the Chinese. 'I will personally go to Beijing and wring his neck,' he thundered.

'Calm down, my friend,' Doshi said, 'I know it is *not* you.'

Hands clasped behind his back, Jha continued pacing the room, alternating between mumbling incoherently to wild shouting and abusing. Doshi knew him too well to say anything further at that time; he let Jha steam off. After a few minutes, when Jha had reasonably quietened down, Doshi got up and poured his friend a glass of water. Jha took a sip, muttered a thanks and sat down.

'How did you...?' Jha left his question unfinished.

'How I knew you are *not* the traitor...' Doshi completed Jha's thought. 'One thing I have learned over the years is that truth, to be accepted, requires time and effort, while misinformation does not. And the Chinese are the masters of deception. Now consider these questions.'

Jha leaned forward in rapt attention.

Doshi continued, 'Firstly, why did Xi call me a few hours *after* the planned attacks were foiled? Did he come to know only later or was he in the know all along? My theory is that he knew about it all along... Sarathi and team have been investigating the Chinese connection for some time now. I would not be surprised if Xi had even commissioned the attacks. But once the plot was unsuccessful, pretending to be India's ally was the best, possibly the only option he had.'

'Secondly, why did he give me the name of the 'traitor'? To mislead me and divert attention from the *real* traitor. Create chaos through misinformation, and buy enough time to think of a way to save the insider.'

'Lastly, why did he give me *your* name? The killing of Raut and Pawar has weakened Adhikari. Imagine if one more strong supporter – *you* – are also out of the picture; alive, but out of the party and politics after being under this cloud of suspicion. That would be the proverbial body-blow to Adhikari. He may have survived the assassination attempt, but would not survive this. And remember, Xi did this without extracting his pound of flesh for the information – albeit, misleading. He is not the kind of man who would give up such an opportunity to get something big out of it. This further reconfirmed my theory.'

Jha raised a finger, as if wanting to pause Doshi and ask a question. Doshi gestured for him to go ahead. Jha asked, 'Let's say if that happened – I mean, Adhikari is out – one way or the other, *you* could have taken over the reins again. You are taking voluntary retirement, but if an emergency such as that arose, it's another matter.' He shrugged quizzically at Doshi, as if he had stated the obvious.

My friend, if you only knew. Maybe the time has come to tell you why I cannot step in. And Doshi told Jha.

When Doshi finished, Jha wept like a child.

***

Only when Doshi insisted that he wanted to rest for a while did a heartbroken Jha leave him. Doshi watched his friend walk away slowly, his shoulders stooped. Doshi felt blessed and sad at the same time.

His thoughts went back to the discussion he had with Jha just minutes ago. Xi had clearly ruled Doshi out of the equation. From not being the killer's target to not seeking anything from Doshi during his call. And that meant only one thing.

Xi knew that Doshi had little time to live.

57

Doshi's thoughts were interrupted by a tapping sound. He waited a few moments to make sure if he had really heard something, when the sound was there again. A soft knocking at the door.

'Come in,' Doshi called out.

The bespectacled figure of a slightly balding, middle-aged man peeped in.

'Oh, it's you. Please come in, doctor, and have a seat,' Doshi gestured to the sofa.

'Did you take the pills in the morning, sir?' Dr Mehta asked politely, yet with a firmness in his tone. Since the previous afternoon, he had been by Doshi's side all along. Now, he was camping next to Doshi's office, ready to jump in if and when required.

'Yes, I did,' Doshi replied, 'thank you for taking so much care of me.'

'It's my job, sir... I just wish there was something I could do to...'

'There's nothing you, or anyone for that matter, can do. We cannot run away from the ultimate eventuality, doctor.'

Dr Mehta nodded, and started, 'Sir, I want to tell you something. I am really sorry about it, and it may mean nothing, but I think it's important I get it off my chest.'

'Go ahead, do not hesitate. I remember you wanted to say something last evening as well... at the hospital.'

'Sir, about your illness... you had asked me to keep it strictly between us, and not let a soul know.'

'Yes, that's right... and?'

'I let it slip once... I had not initiated the topic...and I thought

217

nothing about it, except that maybe I should not have,' Dr Mehta said, his head bowed down.

Maybe this will help me fit the last piece of the puzzle, Doshi thought. 'Don't worry, we are all human, after all. Don't think too much about it... sooner or later, everyone will come to know.'

'Thank you for understanding, sir. And my apologies once again,' a much-relieved Dr Mehta said, talking much faster than usual.

'Just one question. Who did you let know – inadvertently – about my illness?' Doshi asked, looking intently at the physician.

***

Doshi finally knew who the traitor was. He sank down in the armchair, as the revelation hit him. *Was the hate so well-disguised all these years? Was there ever any love and respect? Was the hunger for power so overpowering that one would go to such extremes for it?* He felt his heart exploding with a deep sadness as he recalled a lifetime of warmth and friendship. *All lies.*

Doshi took some time to compose himself, and when he was finally ready, he sat down at his study table and dialled a number. After three rings, the Serpent picked up the phone.

'How are you today, my friend?' Doshi asked.

'I was about to call you. It's been an eventful two days – the attacks... then your hospitalisation. Thank god there was no harm done and all is well again,' the Serpent said, sounding genuinely relieved.

'Are you really thankful about that?' Doshi asked, his tone cold.

'Of course,... what do you mean... I don't understand.'

'I *know.*'

'Now I am really confused.... Know what?'

'I know who the mastermind behind these attacks was,' Doshi said.

'You do? Who is it?' the Serpent said, his voice a pitch higher. a bead of cold sweat trickling down his temple.

'I received a call from President Xi Liu last night... and he told me all about it,' Doshi said. The long silence at the other end reconfirmed his theory.

'I...I don't understand... you know the Chinese well enough not to trust them...,' the Serpent stuttered.

'It's over, my friend. I also spoke with Dr Mehta. Other than him, nobody else knew about my medical condition,' Doshi said, 'and he admitted that he had accidentally mentioned my illness to only one other person... who masterminded this conspiracy. And that person – Lalit Mahajan – is *you*.'

58

Lalit Mahajan, or the Serpent, had waited for years for his efforts and sacrifices to be recognised – and rewarded. Consistently overlooked for key positions, he was left with no choice but to be relegated as the wise old man of the party, who everyone respected and came to for advice, but that was about it.

Every time, when he thought his name would be announced, it was always Doshi's. He always wondered why. What did he lack? Maybe it was Doshi's charisma, or his leadership abilities. *But then, I never got the opportunity to prove myself.* With time, he had tamed his political ambition.

When he learned about Doshi's terminal illness, thanks to a chance, and rather uncharacteristic, slip-of-tongue by Dr Mehta, the ambition that lay dormant within him for so many years, was stirred. He felt he had a real chance; in his opinion, there was nobody else other than him after Doshi. He would still make it past the ultimate finish line. *One last hurrah.* But then came Sanjay Adhikari.

Jha's offhand remark made over breakfast at Davos was the last straw. A decision was made. He would not be overlooked any longer. If, what was rightfully his was not given to him, he would snatch it.

But now, the game was up for him. Mahajan wondered where his seemingly perfect plan went awry. Both his strikes had failed. Even with M dead, he never thought the trail would lead to him. But he had grossly underestimated Doshi; he believed he would never find out. Now it was only a matter of time before Doshi and the party came after him, and that would be the end for him. His political ambitions were dead already, but personally, too, the end was near. Knowing Doshi, a public humiliation, even a charge of treason, was a real possibility. And that is how it would most likely end.

But he had one last card to play. He went to his private chambers, took out the phone from his safe and dialled the only number saved in it.

***

'Your President has thrown me under the bus,' the Serpent hissed, as the man on the other end picked up the phone.

'That's not true,' Chen Jintao said. How was that possible? *He was with the president when the call to Doshi was made. President Xi had called out Namit Jha to the prime minister. Yet somehow, Doshi had figured it all out.*

'You've got to help me now,' Mahajan said.

'Certainly... after all, what are friends for?'

'I need to disappear...for a few months at least,' Mahajan said, his throat dry.

'I see,' Jintao said. He was in no mood to do anything for the Serpent. But if Mahajan were to open his mouth about the hand Jintao had played in the whole botched-up operation, it would be curtains for his own career; and global embarrassment for his country. In all probability, Xi would make him pay for it with his life. Jintao quivered at the thought, and returned to his call. 'I will arrange that – just do as I tell you.'

***

In less than an hour after speaking with Jintao, Mahajan left his residence. Wary of what plans Doshi would have already set in motion for him, he refused his official car and driver. He also smiled and declined his security cover, and chose to drive his private car. 'Just going out for some fresh air. I'll be back in an hour,' he told his entourage.

Following Jintao's instructions, he headed straight to the Chinese embassy in Chanakyapuri, and reached the back entrance. As soon as he arrived, the guard pressed a button to open the electronic grilled door. Mahajan was pleased he did not have to wait; Jintao had made all the arrangements, as promised. He did not notice that the only security camera located outside the embassy's rear entrance was pointing to the sky.

Mahajan was thinking about Jintao's offer as he got down from his car at the service lobby, and was escorted into the embassy by two agents waiting for him. Within an hour, he would be on a private flight to Beijing, where Jintao would receive him. And within the next few days, he would get his own private residence in Chaoyang. Not as good a deal as Khorgos, but given the situation, it was a deal Mahajan would have to make do with. And for Doshi and this country, Lalit Mahajan would have disappeared from the face of the earth.

The two agents led him down a grey, dimly-lit hallway. The reception and the small office area leading to the hallway were empty. Mahajan looked at his watch and wondered where everyone was. *It was too late for lunch.* As they reached the end of the corridor, one of the agents pushed open a metal door, and held it open for Mahajan. The room was dark and windowless. There were two more agents waiting inside. One of them came towards Mahajan and forced him to sit down on the only chair in the room. While he held him down, a second agent taped his mouth, and the other two, using a metal wire, tied his hands to the arms of the chair.

Mahajan, seething with anger, struggled to free himself. One of the four men left the room, closing the door behind him. Thoroughly confused at this turn of events, Mahajan looked pleadingly at his captors. *Surely there was some mistake, he just wanted them to speak with Jintao once.* The men stared expressionlessly at him, and one of them put on music on his phone. Listening to the music, the three smiled. Just then, the door opened and the fourth man returned. When Mahajan saw the bone-saw in his hands, his eyes grew wide with fear. He started trembling violently, and his wrists were bloodied as he struggled against his metal chains.

The man with the bone-saw continued listening to music as he powered the saw, and moved towards the captive man.

59

One year later

The clouds had cleared after a week of heavy rains, and the sun shone brightly over a thankful city. Anant stepped in through the gates of Bada Kabristan, as he had done every week for the past one year, and walked slowly along the grassy path. The ground had a softness to it, and there was dew on the surface. He passed another group of mourners; a loved one being laid to rest with a promise of not being forgotten, but it was a promise that was always broken. *He would not break it.* He recalled the details of that day better than any other day; it was branded into his memory.

At the far end of the city's largest cemetery, upon the stretching green, lay a tombstone identical to the countless others. Yet, as Anant knelt down and kept the flowers at it, he felt a lump rise in his throat. A tear escaped his eye as the name etched upon the headstone spoke to him. *Ashraf Siddiqui.*

Anant stood in silence, reliving the moments he had spent with Ashraf. *His friend. A good man if ever there was one, who gave up his life to protect others.*

'Till we meet again, brother,' Anant caressed the engraved name, and walked out of the gate. He smiled as he saw Nandini wave out to him from the car. He waved back with both hands; he was feeling lighter already. Nandini was coping well, and the doctors had termed her recovery as 'rare', if not a miracle. Anant didn't care what the reason was; he was just glad she was *with him.* He had offered his resignation to spend time with her, but it was rejected outright by Sarathi, so he had settled for a sabbatical instead.

He sat down at the driver's seat, held Nandini's hand, and said a silent prayer. A pair of tiny hands went around his neck, accompanied by squeals of joy. He turned around and gave a high-five to Naima, who returned it with a wide grin, her dimples sinking deep into her cheeks. *One day, I will tell you what a hero your father was. I will keep him alive for you. Always.*

'So, who wants to have ice cream?' Anant asked his girls.

'Meee!' the two passengers screamed together.

Epilogue

In spite of a rising global concern and frequent accusations that the Belt and Road Initiative was neo-colonial, China continues undeterred in its quest to become an economic superpower. India remains one of the few countries that has openly opposed the BRI, maintaining its refusal to sign an agreement with China.

Chen Jintao resigned from his post as China's foreign minister, citing personal reasons. A week later, he was found dead in his mansion, apparently shot point blank during an armed robbery gone awry. The case was closed, and forgotten, after a hurried investigation.

Sanjay Adhikari became the fifteenth prime minister of India, succeeding Mahendra Doshi, who succumbed to a terminal illness three months after Adhikari was sworn in.

Anant and Nandini adopted Naima, but it was the little girl who gave them a fresh lease on life.

The Serpent's disappearance remains a mystery till date. The truth about the role he played in the assassination plot, revealed by Doshi, stayed alive with Adhikari. The prime minister continues to be on his guard, not knowing when, and how, the Serpent will strike again.